C0-AAP-020

CIRCUITS & STEAM

FATES PRESS

CIRCUITS

STEAM

THREE FATES PRESS

Circuits & Steam

Copyright © 2014 3 Fates Press

Each selection herein © 2014 by the author or artist

ALL RIGHTS RESERVED

No part of this book may be reproduced or transmitted in any form or by any means, electronic or mechanical, including photocopying, recording, or by any information storage or retrieval system, without prior written permission from the copyright owner unless such copying is expressly permitted by federal copyright law. The publisher is not authorized to grant permission for further uses of copyrighted selections printed in this book. Permission must be obtained from the individual copyright owners identified herein. Requests for permission should be addressed to the publisher.

Published by 3 Fates Press, LLC, 2025 Bell Rd. Morgantown, IN 46160

Cover art by Jordan Bell

ISBN 978-1-940938-33-2

This is a work of fiction. Names, characters, places and incidents are products of the author's imagination or are used for literary purpose and are not to be construed as real. Any resemblance to actual events, locales, organizations, or persons, living or dead, are entirely coincidental. The names of actual locations and products are used solely for literary effect and should neither be taken as endorsement nor as a challenge to any associated trademarks.

CIRCUITS & STEAM

CONTENTS

CIRCUITS

STEAM

CIRCUITS

Quick Pix
Brick Marlin

Everyone else was doing it, so, why not she?

Allison strolled out of one of the many One-Stop-Shop-Medical-Specialists (OSSMS) parlors in the city, immediately using her new camera eye, the 35mm Turbo. By tapping her temple, she snapped her first picture of a small boy holding a balloon in the shape of the lovable Spencer the Spider from the show, Arachnophobial Dreams.

Her operation had been quick, painless, lasting less than an hour; much less than when she had to replace her lower jaw due to an extreme case of TMJ.

Recalling that memory gave her a touch of frustration; not only because she didn't care for the MS's halitosis, but felt as if she'd been ripped off. Her jaw had begun to pop again and her teeth began their grinding again while she slept — more so now than before the procedure.

Sighing, she knew she'd have to pay a visit to the fake quack soon, using the extended warranty the stupid clone sold her. Why couldn't actual specialists be on staff, instead of staying on vacation three hundred sixty five days out of the year? Allison felt that government should create a law to limit how many clones are made in the world.

At any rate, Allison wanted to shove those thoughts

aside, take a deep breath, calm herself, and move forward. She wanted to enjoy the day using her new toy, never having to use her cell phone for taking pictures again. Sure, she was a bit behind the times, a little late deciding to have the surgical procedure, a little late on deciding to have that pinky removed and replaced with a robotic one that could act like a Swiss army knife and could have very well decided to buy a new improved phone — or a nanobot that would crawl inside your ear, attaching itself to the ear drum, becoming an inner phone (IP) — but she'd still have to poke at the camera app on a 3D hologram in front of her eyes. Plus, there were people who complained that their ear constantly itched. One case involved a customer's ear bleeding.

The 35 mm Turbo was a more efficient way of taking pictures. Downloading them into her home PC tablet by connecting a cord to the USB port right behind her ear would be a snap.

Passing by a waste depository cylinder with flashing yellow words ONLY YOU CAN PREVENT CITY WASTE IN DEPUTY POINT! written on the side, a man dressed as a clown strolled along and gave her a black wink and a red smile. It made her shudder. She wasn't a clown fan, that's for sure. Her brother tormented her enough when they were little, reading scary stories about robot clowns wielding axes.

Since the invention of other OSSMS locations for people who decided to have permanent clown makeup tattooed into their faces, like this guy, she felt the world was nose diving into the Ohio River without an oxygen mask or hazardous waste suit.

Allison decided to make a trip to the park before the sun took its rest for the evening, and snap pictures of the landscape. After arguing with her vehicle regarding which direction to travel, this vehicle being infected with the Tourette's Symptom Virus that constantly complained and vocalized a few choice phrases, she arrived at Deputy Point Sanatorium Park and Play.

The car slid its door to the side, told her to get the hell out.

Allison huffed. She wasn't going to let a stupid machine ruin her day, and she sure wasn't going to take the time to plug the cord into a nearby outlet so the titanium defect could charge its battery. Let the Martian-made piece of crap use its reserve cells for the drive back to her apartment!

Allison chose a dirt trail and followed it into the woods. Every so often, a neon-green holographic cross would be suspended in the air, posting some of the many spots where murders and suicides took place when patients had escaped from the sanatorium five years ago, closing it down permanently.

One hundred years before that, it housed tuberculosis patients.

Allison stepped over a fallen branch and noticed a ghost hanging by a noose on another tree, swaying back and forth without a breeze blowing. The ghost was smiling for a man who stood there taking the picture with his cell phone. A few feet away, she stepped behind a woman also using a cell phone to take pictures of her child standing next to two apparitions repeating a murder scene: a patient repeatedly sinking the blade of his hatchet into a nurse's face.

Allison didn't exactly understand the nature of that one. She really had no need to be around or take a picture of a ghost killing another ghost.

Nowadays, ghosts were sanctioned off in particular spots, such as this place, forbidden to leave the premises to haunt houses or harm mortals, unlike in the past, when people had to eventually vacate their homes from the infestation of the paranormal.

Times had changed.

She climbed a small hill, and soon had a great view of a lake. A group of kids took turns throwing rocks through the body of a ghost who repeated his suicide over and over by walking into the lake, allowing the water to cover his six-foot-tall body from head to toe. Other visitors to the park used hover boards and jet skis, careful not to run through face-down apparitions littering the surface of the water.

Most used it as an obstacle course.

Allison snapped photos of people having fun, with the addition of the suicidal ghost suddenly turning tail and taking chase after the kids who had been throwing rocks through him. Under paranormal laws, the ghost was forbidden to touch them, though it gave the kids quite a scare.

Satisfied, Allison headed back to the car. She had to not only argue for it to slide open its door, but argue for it to start its engine. Tuning out curses from her vehicle during the drive back home, she opened her compact mirror to make sure no dirt was on her face.

A thought pulled up a stool, sat down, and poked at her frontal lobe.

Holding the mirror away, reflecting her entire face, she snapped a picture.

Ha! She loved taking pictures of herself! This. Could. Be. Awesome!

Allison hurried past another freak, a mime bleached

white, who tipped his fedora hat at her, and opened the door to her apartment. She whistled a few bars of the song "Pure Imagination" from Willy Wonka & The Chocolate Factory for her lights to come on, watching the automaton roaches scatter — the ones she did not know were charged up and ready to go when she opened the package from The Joke's On You! Internet store — and whistled part of the "Oompa Loompa" song for the small black box on the wall to project the hologram of the TV series Who Was Stupid Enough To Eat The Polka Dotted Pickle On The Floor Long After The Five Second Rule?

Listening to the audience laugh at the actors making bad jokes, offensive ones at that, she told the TV to switch to the Discovery Channel. The show displayed a local factory that built robots. A man named Baron Fields narrated the segment, explaining in detail about how automatons are constructed, and what great use they have been to humanity.

Allison wasn't sure if she'd ever purchase a robot or not; perhaps when she had saved more money, or got a raise.

Riiight.

She walked into her bedroom, changed clothes, catching a glimpse of herself doing so in the mirror. She smiled. She had another idea. Tapping her temple, she began taking pictures leaning against the wall, crossing her eyes, sticking out her tongue, acting the goof, lying on the bed. Too bad she didn't have a boyfriend. She could really get inventive, emailing provocative pictures!

When was the last time she had a date?

Geez! That long ago?

Allison switched on her tablet computer, connected the

cord to her USB port, and downloaded her pictures. Scanning the gallery, the picture of the boy with the balloon popped up first. The scenes from the park captured the actions of all the people who were having fun. The pictures looked professional.

Allison thought they were awesome! Her cell phone's camera ability could actually be considered behind the times.

Flipping through more pictures, she noticed something odd. Black spots appeared in a few. Allison wasn't sure if maybe there was a glitch in her 35 mm Turbo, or if it was the glare of the sun. Shoving the oddity to the side, she checked out more pictures, finding not only more spots, but the face of a skull. Not sure what to think about it, pawning it off as an apparition not entirely formed, a yawn snuck up on her. She decided that the oddities in the pictures weren't anything to worry about and looked at two more photos — two she knew for a fact had no other black spots or a skull in them — and saved the files.

The evening was getting late. Work arrived early. She did not need another occurrence in her employee file; three more and she'd be out the door. So she retired for the evening, whistling "Pure Imagination" once for the lights to wink out, and dreamed of an odd carnival with vampires, werewolves and zombies as the main attractions.

⊛ ⊛ ⊛

At the office, the daily test given by corporate arrived bright and early. The clone of a tall handsome man wearing cologne made a pass at her to find out if she would try and flirt back. Since she knew it was a test and knew this was pure stupidity from her employer — one would have to be an idiot to fall for such a thing — she told the clone to stay away from her or she would run to HR.

She sat down at her desk and logged into her email to find she already had a message from Management, praising her, saying that she passed the test and would receive a point toward a gift out of the catalogue.

The day cruised by unscathed from enduring too much stress. Afterward, Allison tricked her car into thinking they were going to a local Jiffy Lube Express for an oil change, just so she could slip into the small café next to it.

Her car shouted a few choice words when it noticed her hurrying toward the cafe's doors, making a passing couple wearing brightly colored shirts and retro parachute pants frown.

Allison ate her supper. Using her compact mirror, she took pictures of herself drinking a beverage with a yellow curly straw. A picture of a smiling turtle holding an umbrella hung on the wall a few feet behind her. On its umbrella another turtle did the same, making the picture recursive. She had the ability to post it on Facebook Max, via Wi-Fi from eye to cell phone app. She wished she could figure out how to do the same when downloading photos into her tablet computer. She usually had numerous "Likes" and comments on her page on a daily basis. Some she had to block because she knew they were more tests from her job.

Great pic, babe!

Wanna see more of your pale flesh, girl!

Red hair is my favorite, Allison . . . especially when I'm thinking about it, bathing in the claw-foot tub, fondling my purple Samurai rubber-ducky!

Corporate tended to bother her more and more these days, for some reason. She guessed they were hinting for her to look for a new job since her contract was six months behind ratification.

She used her phone to scan through some of her friends' Facebook feeds, snapped two more pictures of herself and left.

The ride back home reminded her of when she was in eighth grade, cursed and teased by the kids about her red hair. Now it was her vehicle delivering this message.

She sighed.

She really needed to stop at a local auto shop so they could inject an anti-virus program into her car's system. It wasn't going to be cheap, either.

That night as she sat at home with her tablet computer in her lap downloading her pictures, she now caught shots of not only the face of the skull, but a body taking shape under its chin.

Allison gasped.

The shape was directly under the picture of the turtle with the delightful smile sliced into its face, holding its umbrella.

⚙ ⚙ ⚙

At the office the next day, a clone of a woman rode up in the elevator with Allison, taunting her, calling her names, hoping that she would curse back, knowing that corporate did not allow bad language in the workplace.

Sitting down at her desk, firing up her computer, a message in her email from Management informed her she passed yet another test.

Ugh! Whatever floats their hover craft!

She finished her day once again relatively unscathed, and tricked her car into thinking that it would get an oil change by driving her across town to a small Mexican restaurant. She took pictures of herself drinking a margarita.

The picture hanging on the wall behind her moved on its own, repeating a bullfight. The bull was skewering the matador through his shoulder blade with one of its horns, tearing flesh and clothing, lifting the bullfighter's lips, creating screams.

She snapped more pictures of herself drinking another margarita. The food didn't soak up enough of the alcohol and she nearly stumbled out of the restaurant, only to find that her car had abandoned her.

Geez! I must have really pissed the titanium piece of junk off this time!

She called a cab and returned home, noticing her car parked in the lot in front of her apartment building. It cursed at her when she walked by. She huffed, shook her head, and went into her apartment. She downloaded more pictures and once again noticed the face of the skull, now a completely formed silhouette.

This time it was sitting next to Allison in the booth, back at the restaurant.

A chill crept up, uninvited.

Allison began to wonder if something was wrong with her new improved eye. Was there some kind of reaction to the surgery performed? She was going to have to return to the OSSMS's parlor and find out what was going on.

This was not normal!

❀ ✸ ❀

Allison found the doctor to be about as much help as a sack of broken Jack-In-The-Boxes. The clone informed her no one else had any problems of the like. The only reaction reported was a watery eye; nothing more, nothing less.

Geez! Freaking clones. . . .

She was late for work and had the doctor email HR a

note stating that she was in his parlor, making sure it wouldn't be counted against her. It was unusual that she was not bothered with the taunting of a clone in the elevator before she made it to her desk, logged in, and began her work.

Perhaps Management gave her a free pass for the day.

Five o'clock could not have arrived sooner for Allison. Stress swelled like a green tidal wave smacking into the island of California. People griped at her through Bluetooth about their credit card terminals, calling them nothing more than a toy you'd find in the bottom of a Cracker Jack box. One guy ventured to call her a few choice names, including a few that contained the letters C and T.

Thank goodness for Security sending men to the guy's location, having a one-on-one talk with him using a cattle prod.

Allison ended up walking to Binky's Burgers From Pluto after work, a small restaurant not far from her apartment, because her car had decided to go for a drive and blow off some steam. She took more photos of herself eating a huge burger, ketchup dripping off her chin, and drank a large milkshake.

At home, she again noticed the strange figure in her photos. In some pictures the stranger was nearly blocking her out, sticking its face in front of hers; in another, it used two fingers to make bunny ears over the top of Allison's head.

This had to be some kind of side-effect from her eye, she thought, whether the quack clone doctor agreed or not. End of story. How can something be in her pictures when she had never seen it?

Im-freaking-possible!

She sighed, yawned, shut down her tablet computer

and retired for the night.

❀ ✪ ❀

The next morning, panic entered without knocking.

Allison opened her eyes. She rubbed them, not sure if her vision spoke the truth. The room not only mimicked an old black and white photograph, but the skull-faced stranger in the previous photographs was staring at her.

Its face was colossal; the empty pits for eyes did not blink.

Allison scooted against the wall, feeling like a trapped automaton rat.

The stranger's face pulled backward, exposing unfamiliar scenery colored with green walls and a blood red door. Allison's room shifted and a couple of her pictures fell off the wall, hitting the floor. When things halted their progress, the stranger stepped away, very tall, very gigantic to Allison's view.

It cocked its head, waved once, turned on its heel and stepped through the blood red door.

What the hell was happening?

Allison got out of bed and tried to move forward, only to find an invisible barrier. She used her palms to give it a push, used her shoulder to give it a harder push with a shove, while no-luck-at-all sidled beside her.

She huffed.

She tried her door.

Locked.

Fed up, adrenaline pumping through her veins, she took a run at the barrier, using her shoulder again.

This time she and her bedroom fell forward, the floor reaching up to meet her. She screamed as her world tumbled end over end, lying face-up. The vision she captured was of more pictures on shelves, each one having one or more individuals moving around inside, shouting to be freed.

The room's lighting above winked out, leaving Allison in the dark, listening to the cries and the sniffling and the weeping of the ones trapped in the pictures, like her.

Allison's vehicle drove the skull-faced figure across town to a local OSSMS. The weather man on the radio station said it was a Jupiter-like day — gaseous, lack of oxygen in the atmosphere — and pointed out if you do not need to go out, please, stay inside. The skull-faced figure really had not a thing to worry about.

It was not in its completed mode as of yet.

Since the parlor had not a clone on duty or any other living or breathing thing inside, a hovering robot in the shape of a sphere with one red eye spoke to the customer at the front desk, working out the payment plan to be paid interest-free within a year's time, and fed the photograph of what kind of appearance the customer wanted to have. It led the customer to a booth where four separate jets sprayed a silicone flesh on their frame.

Walking out of the parlor, the first thing she did in her new body was visit a local diner, snapping pictures eating Chinese food.

Later at home, the figure watched Allison, the human who it replicated, hammering her fists against the invisible barrier.

Everyone else was snatching bodies, improving themselves, so, why not it?

She Who Dines
on Heavenly Food

Sara Marian

Picture this. You wake up, glad to find you're in your own bed and not surprised that you're alone in it. The ceiling above you is crumbling plaster and flaking gold leaf, twelve feet high. The tall windows are cracked and missing three of their eighteen panes, which you've replaced with rectangles of colored glass you salvaged. Everything in the room is trying to fall apart, and you spend half your free time trying to prevent it from falling apart.

You're still wearing the club uniform: a black, sleeveless dress that could be construed as sexy if it weren't for the gigantic, lurid butterfly print.

Then you note that the air is filled with the unmistakable smell of burning waffles. It's a familiar smell, but you jerk out of bed — because, even in the lingering stupor of last night's shenanigans, you're vaguely aware of the implications of that odor. Rack your brain and remember being in the lobby, swapping a two-pack of cigarettes from the club for a pint jar of 'shine from Hairy Harry, resident conspiracy theorist and property manager of your apartment building.

If you knew what I knew about the meaning of burnt waffles, you'd have been tempted to stay in bed in the hopes that you wouldn't get caught up in something you didn't understand — assuming it wasn't already too late. You might also have been tempted to rush to the kitchen and confront the perpetrator of the crime against your breakfast — although only if you're either absurdly brave or imprudently temperamental. If you were me, you'd also have felt irrationally concerned about the state of your appearance (particularly your hair), and annoyed with yourself for being worried about it.

Nevertheless, I bolted to the mirror and brushed the tangles out, smacked my cheeks a few times to bring out the color, and picked up a tube of lipstick. After a brief hesitation, I threw the lipstick back into the drawer. Well, maybe. . . . I tossed aside a second shade. He'd notice lipstick, and that would just make things worse.

Forget it! I told myself, and headed for the kitchen.

"Good morning, Miss," he said.

When I say "he," in this instance, I'm referring to Sawtooth Puddingfoot, the most frightening and awe-inspiring butler ever invented. Technically, he was an automaton, but he was such an expensive model it was easy to forget, despite his unnatural height. He looked human, acted (like a weird) human, had human expressions, and had such advanced AI that his feelings were classed as "sentient emotions, not mere simulation" on his creation certificate. Regardless of how expensive he is, there's something severely twisted about Puddingfoot's programming. Whether he was manufactured that way, or whether he started out normal and tweaked his own coding over the years, I couldn't have honestly said.

"I have decided to re-enter your employ, Miss," Puddingfoot announced from about ten feet up.

The butler had been a gift from my rich great-aunt Amelia, who had raised me after The Fall of '63. I used to think that was sweet of her, although I always had an inkling she had reasons I didn't know about. When I'd decided, seven years ago, that no amount of luxury was worth staying barricaded in a mansion with my obnoxious elder cousins, trying to hold off bandit raids for the rest of my life, she'd eventually agreed to buy me passage on a dirigible cruise to what was left of Chicago, but only after she procured Puddingfoot's services. Aunt Amelia's fortune had waned, however. Puddingfoot and I had designed a solar-powered steam engine to help out, Aunt Amelia had scraped up enough money to back it, and my butler had left two years ago to oversee the new manufactory, to our mutual regret and, I admit on some level, to my own relief, as well.

"But I can't pay you," I spluttered, with each syllable finding myself increasingly aware of Puddingfoot's terrifying gaze. His genteel demeanor might fool other people, but I knew him too well to be taken in by his cool and professional manner. He thought with blade-like precision and quantum physics flexibility, and right now he was working on pulling me into some scheme I had yet to discover.

"I was worried about you, Miss," Puddingfoot said, deftly flipping what were once waffles onto a plate. "It has come to my attention that you got into a spot of bother last night at the club."

I knew he hadn't been at the Club last night — had he even been in town last night? — but the image of him, looming in the dim light at the bar, popped into my head. And Aunt Amelia never left our little town in Ohio, so how could she have known to send him? I racked my brain again and recalled the reason for at least part of my disorientation. Sometime between sundown and the transaction with Hairy Harry, I'd sneaked into the opium lounge at the club. Lucky for me, some rich idiot had left five minutes on an opium sim, and I'd plugged it into my arterial input.

Time had narrowed into a thin sliver of immediacy that stretched toward infinity, everything before and after the Now fading to irrelevance.

Within the constraints of my five minutes on the plug, I'd considered the nature of mankind, and decided that we are neither basically good nor evil, but simply adaptive. I'd considered the nature of the universe, and could come to no conclusion except that it is horrifically big. I'd considered myself, and decided not to dwell on the subject. My own inner Dorian Gray is a topic best faced down without wasting a good plug.

My time had run out and I'd pulled the jack, but the effects lingered — would continue to linger for at least . . . whenever I woke up in my own bed, smelling the tragedy of a decent breakfast gone wrong.

I met Puddingfoot's eyes and I knew doom was inevitable on this fine June morning. A buried memory of last night rose to the surface — a conversation between some suits and and myself — but what had been said was lost in the haze of euphoric detachment of the opium plug. Whatever "spot of bother" I'd gotten into, it involved people important at the club . . . people I didn't want to notice me or realize who my family was, who probably weren't above using me as leverage over Aunt Amelia if there was a profit in it for them . . . and I didn't remember a single thing about my encounter with them, except that it had happened.

Even worse, I had a butler again — and no idea what he was up to.

⊛ ⊗ ⊛

After breakfast, things got worse. I'd just laced my boots up over my khakis when I heard a knock at the front door. Out of habit, I headed toward the hallway, but of course Puddingfoot answered. An expletive was followed by a muffled series of scuffling noises and a muted attempt at a scream.

I poked my head around the corner.

"Frank? What are you doing here?"

"Shall I break the arm, Miss?" Puddingfoot offered.

Frank whimpered.

"No, thank you, Puddingfoot, you can let him go."

"A suitor, Miss?"

"I have standards, Puddingfoot. Don't look at me like that!" I snapped, although my butler's expression remained neutral as he loosened his grip on Frank — a neighbor from down the street who tended one of the bars at the Club. "And don't leave me alone with him, either."

"Penelope — who is he?" Frank gasped, edging away from Puddingfoot.

"My butler, Sawtooth Puddingfoot. What are you doing here?"

"You have a butler? We live in the slums."

"I asked what you're doing here, Frank."

"Well, you know, it's Tuesday . . . I was wondering if you had that electrical coffee-maker ready for me?"

"Oh, yeah. Yeah, it's upstairs. Follow me." I led the way out the front door and onto the landing. The stairs spiraled down to a lamplit glow from the lobby; above us, a weak illumination filtered through the dirty skylights. One pane was broken, letting in a shaft of sunlight that pierced the gloom. It also let in rain, of course, and pigeons, so the entire stairwell bore the stains of water damage and bird droppings. Hairy Harry hung and re-hung notices in the lobby and at all the landings: WARNING: TOXIC PIGEONS. DO NOT EAT.

Frank followed me upstairs to the attic, and Puddingfoot kept an eye on him without hovering over us.

When I'd first toured the building, the attic was the deciding factor for me to move in. Along one wall was a bank of low windows overlooking the lake, where half-submerged skyscrapers jutted out of the water. The other two walls were buried behind stacks upon stacks of furniture, shelves, books, trinkets, figurines, watches, speakers, microchips, drawers full of scrap glass and metal, all of it heaped to the roofline. Harry didn't know how to do anything with any of it or what it was worth in trade, so I got the spare key to the attic and full rights to everything it contained in return for a working radio here, a hot plate there.

Frank and Puddingfoot followed me to my little work station by the windows.

"Electrical coffee-pot."

As we headed back down the stairs, Frank spoke up with strained nonchalance. "Penelope, you wouldn't happen to know anything about that explosion in the billiards room last night at the Club, would you?"

"I don't know what you're talking about," I said — and no one ever believes you when you say that, no matter how true it is.

"Oh, I figured you didn't, but I thought I'd—"

"Now why would you think that I would be involved in

anything to do with explosions?"

"Well . . . you did make a weapon out of two bobby pins and the insides of an old television set once."

"That was for a good cause. Do we still have to go in to work tonight?"

"Yeah."

"Huh," I grunted. "Must not have been much of an explosion."

I waited until after Frank left to drop my air of amused disinterest. As soon as I clicked the lock into place behind him, I ran to the kitchen to confront my butler.

"What explosion?!" I demanded.

Puddingfoot obligingly switched on the television set and tweaked the antenna until we had a decent signal for the news channel, although the broadcaster's voice echoed with static.

". . . And now that Reno is officially off the Grid, hundreds of refugees are fleeing the outbreak of riots, raids, and fires spreading throughout the city. We'll have more on that story from our live reporters soon. But first, breaking news from Chicago — it appears that several members of the board of Club Metamorphosis have gone missing after the explosion early this morning—"

I stared hard at my butler, who maintained a stoic interest in chopping up vegetables for whatever he was preparing for my lunch.

A video flashed up over the newscaster's left shoulder. Flames and smoke poured out of the billiards room as a pair of guards drenched the debris-littered hallway with a hose, and sleepy-looking guests stumbled into the edges of the frame, mouthing shouts and exclamations which the news had muted.

"The security team at the resort has refused to disclose any information regarding their investigation into these events," the newswoman said, "and have also refused to cooperate with duly elected law enforcement, who arrived on the scene shortly after the two a.m. explosion."

I leaned forward to get a better look at the footage. Was there a figure in the smoke, or. . . ? What time had I left the club? Had I even been there at two a.m.? I was pretty sure that, if that was a figure in the smoke, it was much too tall to be me.

The news moved on, and I switched off the set.

"Are you going to explain?" I asked.

"Not at present, Miss. Would you prefer your stir-fry over rice or noodles, Miss?"

I spent most of the afternoon working on carving a new font for my homemade typewriter — good, steady work that left my brain free to float where it pleased — but my memories from the previous night still hadn't cleared up by the time I changed into my Club Meta uniform. Emerging from the musty lobby into the breezy late afternoon, I felt truly awake for the first time all day. The streets in my neighborhood were lined with sturdy brick buildings whose ornate facades spoke of better times, and the occasional burnt-out shell that had crumbled in on itself peered out from between its neighbors as if accusing humanity of failure to live up to the expectations of those times. Plants had crept through the cracked pavement of the roads and sidewalks, even between the bricks of the walls. Streets lined with clover, walls draped in solid masses of honeysuckle vines, saplings jutting out of intersections. The smell of the lush new growth mingled with the metallic taste of steam on the air, the ever-present musk of decaying wood and plaster lingering underneath.

The slums might be dangerous at night, but, during the day, it was just a neighborhood. I knew more than half of the people on my street by name. People with first-floor access unbolted the doors and sold scrap or sewing, whatever they could scrape together to trade. Somebody was always up on a ladder, repairing the copper pipes or cleaning out a steam valve for their building. Families worked garden patches on the flat rooftops, the kids leaning on the railings and waving at random passersby. I waved back.

The Club board had repaired about half of the old el tracks and replaced the old trains with new steam engines. They tried to pass it off as a community service project, but we all knew better. They wanted business, they wanted workers, and they wanted suppliers. To get alcohol, cigarettes, coffee, drugs, generators, linens, uniforms, carpeting, dishes, food, herbal spa treatments, and all the other commodities nobody else in the city could afford to have all in one place, they had to have transportation to every part of the city — even the slums.

The train puffed to a halt and I stepped on along with half a dozen other people. I found an empty seat next to the window.

On the one hand, it was a good thing for me that the board needed to help the community. On the other, well . . . as Aunt Amelia always said, "Big business is what brought on The Fall. We'd better make sure it stays down if we're gonna rebuild this world."

Funny, I hadn't thought of her saying that in a long time. She'd said it, word for word, just about every day I lived under her roof.

From up here, the city was a maze of interwoven greenery, brick, and steel, the warm sunlight glinting off the new copper pipes and, here and there, intact sheet-glass windows. The occasional isolated overpass, broken off from the old ramps, hovered awkwardly, casting deep shadows over the streets below.

I glanced up and thought I saw Puddingfoot at the end of the car, but, when I leaned away from the bright window to get a better view, there was no one there.

Bad news is good business — when I got to work, the bar was humming with excited conversation, and every customer knew completely contradictory details about the explosion.

Thing is, it's easier to slip out on a busy night than a slow night, because the managers actually have to work. A full tray of drinks and a purposeful stride is the best subterfuge of which a waitress can avail herself in such circumstances.

I slipped into the underlit opium lounge, whose customers were conveniently distracted by the belly dancers onstage, and found Frank tending the bar. I left the tray of drinks with him (my bribe for his silence about my habit) and started my rounds.

When I found a sim with time on it, I glanced around to make sure nobody was paying attention to me. And that's when I caught sight of a trio of people sitting a few tables away, near the stage. One of the ladies from the board sat talking with two guys I'd never seen before. One of them had his back to me, but the other — for some reason — caught my attention. I didn't know him, but somehow he was familiar — like if you saw someone from a wanted poster in real life for the first time.

I felt twitchy. My pulse was so heavy I could feel it in my arms and temples, and I kept having to remind myself to unclench my fists. My vision was fine, but I felt bleary — not tired, but like I was missing every few seconds of time.

One moment, I'm staring at this guy — mid-forties, clean-shaven, sleek haircut that doesn't suit him — and the next moment, he's standing up. He shakes hands with the lady from the board, and then he's gone. I turn around. . . .

And I'm in the hallway, but I don't remember leaving the lounge.

I swear I can hear Puddingfoot's voice, but the words don't make sense to me.

It's dark, a tiny space lit only by a tiny flashlight. I can feel the leather straps of a small backpack on my shoulders. From somewhere, I've gotten a tool set, and I'm opening up a panel in the wall.

I climb the steel ladders inside, two red lines stretching up as far as the flashlight in my mouth will illuminate. It's a long way up, but I feel like I'm gliding along without any effort, every movement precise and silent.

I know exactly where to go, but I don't know how I know.

Wait...did I even get a hit off that plug? I didn't, did I? Then am I actually here, doing this?

I'm in a room, in the dark, hidden. There's a big cut on my left shoulder, four parallel marks that sting, fresh.

I can hear someone coming.

The world has a second chance. I keep seeing my aunt's face, always looking away from me, not meeting my eye.

The room is a bathroom, and it's bright now. Water running in the sink. A mile of mirror stretching out, reflecting the sleek haircut I don't know but I recognize, and he is suddenly startled, his just-washed hands still dripping water as he jumps back.

And in this clean, luxurious room, I find myself standing over him, my shoes in a pool of blood. I don't think he's dead yet, because for a moment our eyes lock, and I know what I've done. I blink, and he's gone, his eyes empty, silent.

I keep seeing my aunt's face, not meeting my eye.

The tile floor is cold under my legs — I'm sitting now, outside of the red puddle. My hands are sticky and dark. And this, too, is familiar. It's happened before.

And I'm thinking, Who am I?

Next thing I know, I'm outside — the balcony, where I launch over the rail without hesitation. I pull a cord on the side of the backpack and hear the rustle and clack of wings unfolding. The parasail catches the wind and lifts, and the city lights spin and drift beneath me. My brain may be chaos, but my muscles are singing, delighted with their own potential.

I know my way home somehow, even though I don't remember when I've flown this route before. I land on the roof of my building and fold in the wings, then slip inside through the broken skylight. Then I'm sitting on the floor in the hallway of my apartment, just inside the front door. It's like I want to be close to the ground so I can make sure it's still really there.

I'm swamped with memories, impressions, fever dreams. Did they happen? Did I even take a hit tonight? I don't think I did.

At least seven individuals stare up from the blackest depths of my memory . . . the red line of my knife blade across their throats, blood surging over the back of my fist . . . before I blink, and they're gone — their eyes empty, silent. The wet gasp for air, the smell of iron. Darkness, where I crawl through to get to them, where no one will see me. Darkness, where I hide so they won't stop me in time. Darkness, where I slink away afterward.

And my aunt? Her fortune . . . her philosophy . . . all of it . . . her eyes never meeting mine. Ever since. . . .

I raise my right arm to look at the input jack. Stare into the small, round empty space that leads to the circuits underneath.

How hard would it be to just rip the whole thing out?

"One's own mind can be a dangerous place, Miss," Puddingfoot says gently, from somewhere above me, "if one dwells there too much and too long." He lifts me, what feels like miles above the chill of the hardwood floor, into his arms and carries me, trembling and twitching against his broad chest.

"Aunt Amelia—" I whisper. "She wired me for this, didn't she?"

"So you know now, Miss." Puddingfoot draws back the coverlet of my bed with one hand and tucks me in place with the other. He pulls a little kit from the bedside drawer and cleans the cut on my shoulder. I watch his face, which shows me nothing. Then he reaches into his pocket and pulls out a portable sim. "This will help."

I hesitate, because everything is a lie. "What am I? Am I a human, or an automaton?"

"A human, Miss, I assure you. However, your cybernetic system is more extensive than you were led to believe."

"She raised me." I remember her love for open windows, the fresh air delivering the intertwined scents of flowers from her garden. And then, when the raids got bad and it was hard to get supplies from town consistently, we boarded up all the exterior windows. In the enclosed courtyard, we ripped up the flowerbeds and planted vegetables, herbs, and berries . . . any food that would grow in our limited space. When we switched the garden over, I checked her expression before I could bring myself to pull the first plant up. She laughed, and we raced each other to see who could tear the garden up faster. "She's using me."

"Yes, Miss."

"And you've been helping her use me."

"I'm sorry to have to say that this is, indeed, the case, Miss."

"She's taking over the Club, isn't she?"

Puddingfoot glances at his wristwatch. "It is highly likely, Miss, that you will receive a phone call within the next four to six hours, in which you will be offered complete control of what has, until this evening, been your place of employment."

"Because I killed people," I say flatly.

"This is true, Miss. Although, if it eases your mind, I can assure you that the individuals in question were of exceedingly low moral caliber, themselves."

"Maybe that'll help tomorrow," I say. I feel numb and panicky at the same time. I realize I'm clenching my blanket in a clammy vise.

Puddingfoot holds out the portable sim again. "In the meantime, Miss, this will help."

I pause for a second, but I want that plug more than anything. Even more than I want answers, even more than I want to erase everything I've just found out.

I plug it in, and finally everything is in focus.

"It raises your dopamine levels, Miss," Puddingfoot explained. "The endorphins block your programming."

"Why—" I started to say, but stopped. There was a weird look on the butler's face. I could've sworn there was genuine sympathy in his eyes.

"Goodnight, Miss," the automaton said, and turned out the lamp by my bedside. "Should you need anything in the night, or feel ill at ease physically, do ring." He shut the door behind him when he left, and I lay staring out the window, watching the moon rise to its zenith, then begin to set, before I finally fell asleep.

Picture this. You wake up, glad to find you're in your own bed and not surprised that you're alone in it. This time, you haven't forgotten what happened last night.

The air is full of the unmistakable smell of burning waffles.

In the hallway, the phone rings, and there's a knock at the door.

"Telephone, Miss."

Excerpt From
Charlotte and Daisy
K.A. DaVur

I crossed to the desk with a dozen eyes fixed on my back, or so it seemed. I am, at the best of times, certain that the word "crazy" is written in giant glowing letters across my back just as it is in the scars on my wrists or the faint burns on my temples. This was not the best of times. I gave my identification number to the receptionist, Cyber, I'm pretty sure, and found a seat at least one empty chair away from anyone else. My sleeves had worked their way up my arms. I pulled them down until the rough fabric brushed against my knuckles, and tried to take the deep, cleansing breaths that Doctor Alyce had said would help. They didn't.

The waiting room was pristine, immaculately decorated, so very different from East, from any of the state run and funded facilities to which I'd become accustomed. Those smell like piss and bleach and are decorated with flaking paint and whatever the last out-of-control patient had smeared all over the walls. Here, everything was cool blues and off-white, with a SimWall depicting a beach or, at least, what a beach used to be. There's a beach down the road from my flat in Flower Town. It does not look like that. Still, the crashing of the waves was nice. Soothing. In and out. Back and forth. In and out. I looked down, surprised to find

I was scrubbing my wrists back and forth on my thighs, and rocking in time with the water. How long had I been doing that? Apparently, a while. The skin was red and the other people waiting to be seen were pointedly not looking at me. Fek.

For some strange reason I thought of Tawny, her dark eyes wide in the dim light while angry footsteps pounded up and down the halls. "You picked a bad time to go loco," she had said. She had been right. That time was bad, this one was worse.

I should just get out of here. They're not going to pick me, anyway; I don't know why I'm even trying. As of right now, I'd be out nothing but the hoverbus fare and maybe, just maybe, I could cling to whatever chip of dignity I had left. If there's any at this point. Sometimes I wonder. Of course, Dr. Alyce would be disappointed. It's not like that's new. I've been disappointing Dr. Alyce for ten years or more, and he's just one on a long, long list; besides, he gets paid to be disappointed, anyway.

My heart started thumping in my chest. I can't do this. I can't not do this. Stay, and people will see. They will see what I am. And, worst of all, they will actually, and this is hilarious, decide that I'm not broken enough or too broken or who knows what.

What if I actually fail at being sick? Go home, though, and there's no hope. None. Besides, they'll all be sitting here knowing I couldn't make it and laugh and talk amongst themselves about the stupid lazy wanna-be patient and how I was probably hung-over or strung out and couldn't find my way. I found my way fine, thank you. Better than they could, if we took them out of their oh-so-pretty world. God, I'm just so damn tired.

I looked again at the SimWall, where a brightly-colored bird was entering from one side. Okay, let the bird decide. If it flew through, just a tourist, I would be on my way. If it stayed, so would I. It soared across the blue sky, banking so that it looked like it was flying away, then curved and came closer, settling on the branch of the tree. All right. I folded my hands in my lap and gave what I hoped was a pleasant smile to the woman across the aisle, and did my best impression of someone who was actually sane.

"Charlotte." Another woman identical to the receptionist was waiting at a door that I hadn't even noticed. So, there's one question answered,: Cyber, for sure. She guided me through a tangle of rooms and hallways, her high patent heels clicking on the tiles. One thing this place did have in common with East, it was a maze. She stopped, finally, and pushed a door open on silent hinges.

"Thanks," I said, forgetting that you don't have to thank a Cyber. She gave me a programmed smile, flashing her flawless white teeth, and clicked back the way she had come. The office behind the door, like the rest of this place, was spotless, beautiful, with real wood furniture and soft fabrics. There were framed awards everywhere. It was obvious they were used to people who were educated, rich. People not like me. I was surprised they even let me in there, probably had a cleaning bot already programmed to sanitize the place after I left. I don't belong here. If they didn't need someone desperate to use as a guinea pig, a place like this wouldn't even answer my waves. Still, Dr. Alyce was waiting, along with two people I had never met. They were all looking at me. I wished that I had left when I had the chance.

Dr. Alyce stepped forward. "Charlotte," he said, clasping my hands in his, "I'm glad you could come. Let me introduce you to our hosts." He turned, first, to the woman on his right, a dark skinned woman with startling hazel eyes and a white coat like his own. "This is Doctor Stevens," he said and, turning to his left, his elbow brushed the elbow of the man next to him and passed right through, leaving a bluish glow behind. The other stranger must have holo'd in for the occasion. The kid, I swear he looked about a decade younger than me, was introduced as Cybernetic Specialist Nu. He wore a dark blue blazer embroidered with the stylized pigeon of the Tesla Academy. A scientist of some sort, then. That explained the holo. I'd heard that most scientists hesitated to leave their labs, afraid that, in the time it took for them to visit the latrines, someone would beat them to the next best thing. I'd seen the T.A. emblem before, of course. Once, on the leg of a drunk, homeless man that we were helping get cleaned up. Mostly, in the hospitals, though. The electroshock machine had T.A. engraved on it, in fact. I wasn't sure what to make of that. I bowed briefly to each, my right hand crossed across my chest, tapping my closed fist on my left shoulder in the true Benevolencia fashion. In other words, the fashion I hadn't used since we learned it in Primary.

"Thank you for considering me," I said.

They bowed in return, perfunctory flicks of the head, and the C.S. motioned to a seat. I sat, caught myself scrubbing at my thighs with my wrists and forced my hands to fold themselves once again. Dr. Stevens made a note in my chart. I felt my gorge start to rise and swallowed several times. Dr. Alyce nodded encouragingly and launched into his prepared speech. We had gone over it together in his office so that I would know what to expect.

"Dr. Stevens, C.S. Nu, this is Patient 3245931B,

Charlotte. I have had the pleasure of working with Charlotte for well over a decade. While her condition is indeed chronic, and, I have reason to believe, progressive, I have found Charlotte to be a willing participant in her recovery." That last phrase I'd heard before, at least a hundred times. I had heard it at each of my Patient Release Meetings. There, it meant that I was going to make it to my appointments, take my meds, and at least try to not to kill myself. I heard it as a joke among the patients at East, our meager attempts at gallows humor. "Now, now," we'd say, when someone sat at the toilet, vomiting their way through the DTs, or the times that someone would descend for a moment into absolute insanity, turning over tables or screaming about spiders that weren't there, "is that a good way to participate in your recovery?" Once, I heard it from three male nurses as the reason that they beat the hell out of Denae, a schizophrenic drag queen and one of my best friends at East. I guess that sounded better than the truth, which is that they got mad when she refused to blow them in the iso room. Those nurses didn't last long, at least. Even the doctors loved Denae.

I came back to now with a start and everyone was staring at me. I must have missed something. Fekegalo.

"I apologize," I said, "I believe I missed the question."

Dr. Stevens scribbled again. A crease had appeared between her eyes. "I asked why you feel that you would be a good candidate for our trial."

Ah. Dr. A had prepared me for this. I launched into our rehearsed speech.

"My disorder reduces my ability to live a normal life. I have a great desire to become a contributing member of society and feel that this procedure would grant me an opportunity to do so. If chosen, I—" The C.S. stifled a small cough. What did that mean? Was it some sort of code? It happened just as I said "If chosen." I lost my place in the speech. Suddenly, the room no longer seemed to have enough air. Harsh, metallic sunbursts exploded at the edge of my vision, leaving dark negatives in their wake. My field of vision shrank, and I felt this straw that I'd been grasping so hard for so long start to slip out of my sweaty grasp.

"I just—" my voice quavered, "I just don't want to feel like this anymore. You don't understand. It's," I tried to choke out the words, words that would explain the constant fear and perpetual loneliness, that could somehow show the pain of stitches and pumped stomachs, of failed relationships and lost jobs, and the constant exhaustion of clamoring and scrabbling at the edge of the pit only to have your fingernails tear off and dirt clods fall in your face but never, ever getting out. I couldn't. "Please," I said at last. "Please help me. I will do whatever you ask. I will follow any plan. I will work hard. Just please. I don't want to live like this anymore." Hot, thick tears built up and overflowed my lower lids. Dr. Stevens was scribbling furiously, though took a moment to wordlessly hand me the box of tissues. C.S. Nu looked studiously at his feet, obviously embarrassed, probably disgusted, at my outbreak.

"Thank you," Dr. Stevens said, "That will be all." The Cyber met me in the hallway, and I expected to be escorted out of the building. If I were lucky, they would have a cab that would take me home. Once there, what? I had been, I knew, at the top of a short list of candidates for this trial. If I had thrown this chance away, like I had so many others, what? I would have to figure out something, but first I thought I would sleep. I was, suddenly, unbearably exhausted. However, when we got to the lobby, the Cyber took me through a door on the other side. There was the feared cab, and in it Dr. Alyce, and together we went to the Facility where the surgery would be performed to give me a new brain and, if they are right, a new life.

March 31st

As of today, I have been at the Facility for two weeks. As soon as I got here, they took me to a room where I sat for hours just filling out forms. I hated it; it was like I had to put my whole disgusting life down on paper for people to see and judge. Education? No high school degree. Parent's current health? I don't know. Father's name? I don't know. Number of times hospitalized? Dozens. Reason? Suicide attempt. Suicide attempt. Histrionics. Suicide attempt. It's all in my record. Do you really need to make me go through it all over again? They had to ask everything in about 20 different ways. I felt so stupid. "Do you understand? Do you understand?" Yes, yes, I understand! You're going to cut out my brain. I imagine there are dangers involved. Then people would walk in and it would start all over again, only they'd talk like I wasn't even there. "Does she understand? Does she consent to? Does she comprehend?"

By the time it was over, I was a wreck, shaking all over and my head was pounding. I couldn't even think. They took me to my room and gave me some lunch. I kept waiting for them to bring my meds, they were way overdue, but they never came. I started asking the nurses, but they wouldn't answer me. Finally, Dr. Stevens and C.S. Nu came in. That's when they told me that they'd be pulling me off of my meds. Cold turkey. You know, it's weird, because I've spent my whole life with people telling me, "take your meds, you can't just stop taking them," and that's exactly what they do. Dr. Stevens insists that that isn't true, that they had meds of their own that were able to combat the withdrawals. I think that's just something that she told me to make me go along with it, because it didn't feel like they were combating anything. I've been so miserable. Endless vomiting, headaches like someone was driving pneumospikes into my brain. Hallucinations. I was apparently convinced that one of the aides was my mother. They had to pull me off of her, or so I've been told. I don't really remember much. And through it all, endless tests. Vial after vial of blood, urine samples, CT scans, head measurements, more blood. I kept asking them to back off just a little. To let me have just a little dose of the meds. To just wait a little bit before poking me again. But, as C.S. Nu keeps insisting, we are on a time frame. The sponsors are ready to move on this, ready to see some results, and are running out of patience. Which is, as far as I can see, another example of the people who have money making life harder for the rest of us. Still, I promised to be a model patient, and so that's what I'm trying to do.

The next step is to get a good "organic map." They need to learn about my personality, what I like and what I don't, how I move and how I think. "We want to make sure that you are still you," C.S. had said briskly. "Just a healthy version. We have no interest in building a robot." I'm not sure that I believe that, but okay. So, that's what I'll be doing the next couple of days, helping them map. That's why I'm keying this journal entry. I have to write one every day from now on, two-thumbing it into a keypad that plugs into a special socket on the bed. Then, they say there are tests. They won't really tell me what they are and I've been sitting here thinking of all the things they could be. I'm scared.

I have to believe that it will be easier than what has happened so far.

April 3

I'm very tired today. I keep trying to take a nap, but that is not allowed. They need to "maximize mapping hours," which means that I have to keep these electrodes, there have to be hundreds of these sensors, glued to my head while we go through hour after hour of these really weird, I don't know, tests maybe? They're not like any test I've ever taken, though. In one of them, I was in a stackflat like the ones down in Flower Town. It could have been one of the ones that I've lived in, I don't know. They all look the same. But anyway, the flats were on fire. The smoke was billowing and I could hear the fire behind me and see the flames sometimes. There were people there, too. I couldn't see them but I could hear them yelling for help. I think that they were trying to see how fast I could get out of there, to see if I could even find my way. So, I just put my head down and ran. I got out pretty quick, so I think I did really well in that one. I had just caught my breath from that when they took me back to my room. They hooked me up to a dozen or more different machines, these in addition to the hell glued to my scalp, and sat me in front of a computer. I don't know how long I was there, answering ridiculous questions, but by the time I was done my eyes were stinging.

That's when I asked, again, to lay down. They wouldn't let me. Instead, they sent in this aide who started asking me all sorts of questions. What I liked to do in my spare time, my hobbies all that stuff. Here I am, sitting in the hospital in a gown and my underpants, my head shaved, shaking and trembling and exhausted and they send in her? She looks about twelve, like she's never had a care in the world. Her voice is like a bird chirping. I wonder how much they had to pay her to pretend to be my friend. I can just imagine what she's going to say to her friends tonight, how she had to spend time with this disgusting freak. I hate what they've done to me here. It's like they took a magnifying glass and made all of my issues bigger, even more out there. I thought I was coming here to get better? So, I couldn't get her to understand that I don't have hobbies. I don't have things that interest me. One way or another I spend my time trying to survive. I work to try to have a place to live. I go to that place and sleep. If I can't fall asleep, if the worries and the memories and the nightmares get to be too much I find something to distract myself enough so that I don't end up in the hospital again. Do I read? Yes. Well, what? I don't know. The words are usually jumbled on the page and I'm too weary to try to figure them out. Do I watch television? Yes? What do I watch? Whatever is on. I forget what show I'm watching while I'm watching it. After a while, a nurse came in and told me I had to get dressed, that we were going to try something else. So they gave me some clothes and a wig to cover the electrodes, and put me in these special glasses that made me look like a freak. Then they took me to one of the giant shopping malls over in the luksa part of town. I'd never been anywhere near there before.

Seen from above, the city looks like a bull's-eye or a rock tossed in the water, with the Palace in the center and all the neighborhoods spreading out in rings. The best neighborhoods are in the center, all the way down to us in Flower Town on the harbor and the factories to the North. So, they dropped me off with an aide and told me to do whatever I wanted. What I wanted to do was sit by the fountain in the middle of the lobby, the one that shot all of these multicolored jets of water, and pretend that people weren't staring at me and maybe doze a little bit. I guess that wasn't the right answer because the aide started chirping at me about getting an "accurate map." I asked how it could be accurate if they had me doing things that I never did in real life. The aide walked off and soon Dr. Stevens was on the phone. She started talking about how she was concerned if I was really willing to put in the work necessary. I still didn't understand, but I got up and followed the aide around while she showed me all of the things that were for sale.

"Do you like these?" she asked, and pointed at these enormous wigs and dresses you could program to look like any fabric you could imagine. "How about these?" to a rack of helpbots; there was one that would cook you dinner, one that would paint you a picture. I shook my head. "Well, what kind of things do you like?" she asked. I shrugged. My head was starting to hurt. We left shortly after that. I hope they learned something, because I'm exhausted. I asked if they could take just a few of the electrodes off, the ones just behind my ears itch like crazy, but apparently there's some pretty important parts of the brain just behind your ears. I keep telling myself that it's all going to be worth it, but I don't know anymore. It's starting to seem like some big joke, like this can't possibly work. Right now, I'm just waiting to sleep. They say I have a few more tests. So, I'm just going to hang on a little longer.

April 4

Diable, I was wrong. They finally let me lay down after

dinner, so long as I was willing to listen to a recording of the news until I fell asleep. That was fine. After a while, I didn't even notice it. But then I couldn't get comfortable. The sensors were pulling on my scalp, which was itchy as hell anyway because my hair is starting to grow back in. I kept calling the nurses and asking for them to give me something, but they said I just had to try to deal with it. So I tossed and turned and eventually I fell asleep and then I had nightmares all night long. They were obviously from those stupid tests because I was back in the stackflats and they were on fire. This time, though, it was my mother and sister who were screaming for me. Which is weird because, except for that hallucination, I haven't thought of them in forever. But anyway, Instead of trying to get out, I was trying to find them, and there were all of a sudden hundreds of doors. I was opening them as fast as I could, one after another, but I couldn't find them. Finally, I would open the right door and there they would be, Mother with her long hair and Daisy, my sister, tiny and dark-eyed and still six years old just as she was the list time I saw her. How long has it been? A decade? More? I would be trying to get to her and save her but Mother wouldn't let me. Her hands were on fire and she was hitting me with them telling me that the fire was all my fault. I'd be fighting her still while the skin blackened and melted off of her bones, still fighting until the explosion brought me to shivering, gasping wakefulness.

I must have watched them die a dozen times last night and was still feeling shaky and raw when they led me through the corridors and stairways that made up this sterile maze. Up and down, left and right until finally we ended up in what they called the Nursery. As it turns out, my nurturing levels are very low. Like, almost non-existent, which I guess makes sense when you think about it. It has been more than I can handle just to take care of myself; I sure haven't spent much time worrying about taking care of anyone or anything else. Turns out, though, the ability to nurture is, how did C.S. Nu put it? "Necessary to optimal psychological well-being." So, I'm going to need to learn it.

At first, I freaked out a little. I thought they were going to make me, I don't know, be an aide here in the hospital or Godhelpme, have a kid of my own. Thankfully, it's nothing like that. All it means is that I had to pick out a Cynimal. So, we opened the door and here were all of these animals crawling and flying around, screeching and barking and whatever. It was way too much for me and I had to leave. So, they found this little room for me and brought the Cynimals to me one at a time. I told them they could just pick out whatever one they wanted, but they wanted me to decide. So I played fetch with a dog for a while and fed fake crickets to a lizard, but neither of them really did it for me. The chimp creeped me out, it was just too much a like a human and we had to stop for a little while while I got myself back under control. The miniature elephant weirded me out, too. Like, I know none of these are real, but that seemed too much like a toy. I kept picking it up and turning it upside down and eventually I guess I stressed it out because it just powered down. I asked for a cat, but I guess even programmed cats don't really make you nurture them, which is why I had asked in the first place. Finally, I decided on a rat, mostly because I was still thinking about all of my dreams from last night and the rat was tiny and dark and big-eyed and it reminded me of my sister. I even named the thing Daisy. So they're going to grow or build or hatch or whatever they do to my Daisy, and I guess she will be ready by the time I come out of recovery. It might be kind of cool, maybe. I never had a pet before.

April 6

I knew today was going to be important when C.S. Nu came to see me in person, instead of holoing himself in. I don't think that he would ever leave his lab if he didn't have to. Even the nurses agree. I overheard two of them talking one day when they brought the holo projection screen into my room.

"That man would holo himself to take a shit," one of them said, and they laughed. I laughed, too, and it must have scared them. They don't really think I'm a person, and it upsets them when I actually act like one. Just lay there, don't think. Don't ask questions. Just do what I tell you to do. They say they don't want a robot, but I think they kind of do. Either that or they think I'm stupid, or not worth taking a minute of their time to actually treat me like a person. Maybe they're right. God knows I've thought the same thing before. Useless. Worthless. Waste of breath. Toxic. Poison. Still, it would be nice if they would, I don't know, actually acknowledge my presence. Anyhow, I laughed and they got quiet. I think the C.S. Is probably a bit of a kacisto when he's not hungering for the opportunity to hack out your brain.

As it turns out I was right, about it being important, not necessarily about the C.S. being a kacisto. My procedure is scheduled for tomorrow. They figure that they will have all of the mapping done that they need to do by noon. My new brain has already been grown; they did that with all of the tissue and blood samples that they took, and now they just need to program it. They say that I should be able to have my sensors taken off after lunch, and then take a shower shortly after. They also told me to think about what I might want for dinner tonight. They said that I could pick anything that I wanted and they would bring it to me. At first, I couldn't think of anything special, and I was going to ask them just to bring me up whatever they were serving down in the cafeteria. Then I thought I might ask for something really fantazio, something I could never have any other time, like a real steak from a real cow, not synsoy. Finally, though, I decided on some soup and a sandwich from Don's Cafe over in Flower Town. Partially because I thought it would be pretty funny, seeing someone from this place trying to walk down the streets of my home. Mostly, though, because I had spent what was, looking back, the best two years of my life working there, and living in the flats above. I started out with the most basic stuff, stocking the pastry case and pouring the ready-made soups into the pots to heat. Soon, though, Don promoted me to baker. It was the first time I'd been promoted to anything. I loved it. The smells, the reliability of the recipes, the rhythm of kneading the dough. It was all very soothing to me, gave me a feeling of accomplishment. You do something right, it turns out good. The way life should be, but isn't. I let Tawny move in with me as well, she and Dmitri, her on-again/off-again boyfriend. Dmitri worked long hours down by the harbor, and would come in smelling of oil and the sharpness of seawater. Tawny and I would hoot him down, laughing and taunting until he showered off the worst of it, then we'd settle in for the evening, laughing, smoking, watching movies on the ancient flat screen that Dmitri had hauled home proudly from the hock shop one night. Even at our most flush, we never had enough for a SimCenter. Sometimes, Dmitri would drag out his guitar and we'd sing along, but mostly we would just sit together dreaming our dreams. They were good days, the best, and, while I never had anyone serious, I even dated now and then. The nightmares stopped, my scabs healed, and, thanks to then endless stream of breads and pastries, I even grew a thin layer of flesh over my perpetually skeletal body.

But it had to end and one night it did. It was fall, the period between the stinking heat of summer and the bitter cold of winter, when Flower Town is actually bearable. People had been throwing parties all up and down the streets for weeks. Finally, it was our turn. It seemed like the whole neighborhood showed up to dance and drink and eat the mountain of goodies that Tawny and I had baked. I'd gone off my meds the week before. I'd been doing so well and thought that, maybe, this time, it would be all right. I'd also started drinking early, trying to combat the anxiety that came with the guests. By the time guests started to arrive, I had overdone it and was starting to feel a little on edge. I spent most of the night hiding in the corner, breathing deep and nursing a beer, smiling a little whenever anyone came close. Sometime around midnight, Chandra, who makes a living busking on the street, telling fortunes, decided to start reading palms. It was pretty funny at first; she told Dmitri that he would end up married with three children. Dmitri yelled and gave her the evil eye. She told someone else, a guy whose name I can't remember, only that he was a nephew twice or three times removed, and thus in the employ, of a local mobster, that he'd someday be working in Capital City, itself. Then it was my turn. I tried to refuse, but everyone chimed in, chanting my name and "oh come on" until finally

I gave in.

Chandra took my hand, and her smile disappeared. His brows knit together. "Oh, Lotta," she said softly. "Death, death and destruction."

"For me?" I asked.

She nodded. "For you, for everything you touch. You have the broken knot." She ran her long, psychedelic nail over a place in my palm where the creases came together for a brief moment before racing off in different directions. "What is broken cannot be saved."

The room started closing in then, and I heard a noise, a high, piercing, endless howl that it took me a full minute to realize was coming from my own mouth. I started to claw at myself then, at least I was told, and managed to leave long deep scratches down both cheeks and one arm before they were able to stop me. It took three big guys to hold me down. They pinned me for hours, but every time they would let go, I would start again. Once, I ran for the balcony. Another time, I made it as far as the kitchen and the butcher knife we kept there. Finally, at dawn, not knowing what else to do, the people who hadn't already freaked out and bailed loaded me up and dropped me, at Tawny's instructions, back at East. I was there that time for six months. Still, two years was a good run, the best that I've been able to expect, really, and Don has been great since then about giving me a job at the cafe when he thought that I could handle it, and food when he didn't.

You know, they told me that I could have visitors tonight, but I couldn't think of anyone that I could ask. I wish I'd thought of Tawny and Dmitri. I'd like to see them one more time, if. . . . Just if. It's too late now, though. I don't even know where they live. Maybe I'll record them a letter. One that Dr. Alyce can deliver, if he needs to. In the meantime, soup and a sandwich. Roast beef synsoy, extra Swiss, horseradish and cherry compote, maybe on that nice dark bread I used to make, the one with all of the seeds baked on top. That sandwich was my own creation, they called it Little Lotta. And whatever soup they have today. Yeah. That's what I want. That would be nice.

April 7

As it turns out, the surgery is not going to be today. I'm not even sure right now, they aren't even sure, if there's going to be a surgery at all. I lost control last night, to the point that they had to sedate me. I just, I got to thinking, "What if this doesn't work?" I don't mean what if I died. The thought of death doesn't bother me, hell I've tried to get there on my own; would have, if I actually had the courage. Turns out I'm even a failure at that. But what if it doesn't work and things stay exactly the same as they are right now? What if it's just like everything else that they said would work and that hasn't worked and then I'm right where I am now only then there's no hope? This is it. This is the bottom of the barrel. After this, there is nothing, and so if this doesn't work that means that I will stuck feeling like this for the rest of my life and I can't. I just, I can't bear the thought of that. So I was sitting here in the dark, by myself, thinking of all those years with no hope and it just got to be too much. Eventually, they had to sedate me and I guess that they can't do the implant if I've had a sedative so we have to wait until it's out of my system before we can go on. Then there's Dr. Stevens. I don't think that she's ever liked me much and now she does not want to use me at all. I was only picked because Dr. Alyce and C.S. Nu thought that I was best. Dr. Stevens had someone else in mind. Not that they told me that but, like I said, people talk.

But here's the thing: you pick someone for a surgery because they aren't well, because they can't cope with life like other people can, then you get upset when they can't cope. That doesn't make any sense. If I could deal with stuff, I wouldn't be here in the first place, letting them cut out my brain. Would anybody do that if they thought they had any choice whatsoever? It doesn't mean I won't work hard. It doesn't mean that I won't try, that I can't be real, I can't be right. It just means that I need help. So why won't they help me? How can they get my hopes up and then just leave me out here alone? How could I possibly go home knowing I was this close to being normal, that I was this close to being okay, and then I just threw it all away? That they took it all away for me for having the sickness that brought me here? I can't. I can't do that. I just can't. Here they are now. I hope its good news. Please let it be good news.

Queen Jeshica

Thomas Lamkin Jr.

The newest luxury liner airship was pulling into town tomorrow afternoon, and tickets were half a working man's yearly pay. Jeshica didn't work, and she wasn't a man, but she knew she had to be on that ship. The Melpomene was on posters all over town, glorious and huge as it came through a cloud bank toward the viewer. The yellowed papers had caught the eye of the vagrant community, and the most brave or most desperate had seen their escape in that fancy dirigible.

Jeshica tucked the discarded poster into one of her many pockets and pried herself out of the small hole in the wood-slatted wall. New Chicago wasn't the worst city, she thought to herself as she checked her arms and legs to be sure the scratches she'd earned were not bleeding. Under all the polished brass and bronze, copper domes and sparkling gas lamps, that's where you could see the heart of the city. Jeshica emptied her other pockets of trinkets and bits of scrap. The usual small crowd of other vagabonds waited impatiently for her to emerge from the hole through which only she could fit. Dirty hands reached out of ragged sleeves, and the treasures disappeared. She reached out and grabbed at one wrist, meeting the eyes that peered out from under a broad-brimmed hat that had seen better days.

"For supper. Not for free.

The man nodded and hurried off, taking away the little bits that Jeshica had recovered from the narrow passages of what they called The Pile. Under New Chicago lay the bits and pieces of older versions of the city. More and more was built on top of it until people forgot about the catacombs, tunnels through old buildings, and, somewhere down at the end of all the sewers, a lake. The lake that rumors said stretched north like a mirror beneath the clouds.

⚙ ⚙ ⚙

"You won't be able to do this forever," one of the crones said as Jeshica stood and brushed grime and rust off of her trousers. "You'll be too big, and you'll have to stop, or get stuck," she rasped. Jeshica caught the undertones of jealousy. The woman was hungry, and this willowy girl's ability to trade her finds for food was insulting. By the look of her toothless grin, she was looking forward to the latter option. Jeshica already felt stuck, which is why she refused to hand over the poster. "Or keep singing, little Jeshica," and now the woman stepped closer. "And see that the'ill start wanting more than your voice. You've hidden this long, but they'll notice. He'll notice. . . ."

With a juke to the left, Jeshica shot to the right and around the old woman, leaving her cackling laugh to echo down the alley behind her.

As far back as she could remember, Jeshica would stand under the gaslight and sing for whatever coins she could squeeze out of the poor passers-by, or the occasional well-to-do stranger who had taken a shortcut through her neighborhood on his way to somewhere cleaner. But the crone was right. As she began to blossom as a woman, her songs were not the focus of attention any longer. She struggled to continue singing, pretending not to notice the added attentions, but soon it became obvious that the coins were a prelude to encourage her to do more than sing. Extra money was offered for her to come away quietly. Jeshica was not unique; she had seen this happen to other girls. Often it happened to them sooner, because they had nothing else to earn coin except to make themselves into women before their time. She always assumed that one day her voice would not be enough.

As she dodged through another alley, Whistler grabbed her wrist and the future she expected was swept away.

Whistler was another with a musical bent, to the point that his actual name was lost years ago. He had perfected the ability to purse his lips and make two notes at once, and his unique talent was what kept him with enough coin that even his scraggly white goatee was somewhat well-groomed. The old gentleman always had a bemused twinkle in his eye, like he was in on some joke and was just waiting to tell you. He was also a very gentle soul. Now, however, his grip on Jeshica's wrist was insistent and that twinkle had become a hard glint.

She started to protest, but the way his eyes narrowed made him look fierce. Dangerous. Jeshica had never thought of Whistler as dangerous. She swallowed the taste of acid.

"You got family, girl?"

Jeshica shook her head, confused and suddenly afraid of her old friend. "You know I ain't, Whistler. What—"

Whistler's face wrinkled further in a frown and he looked both ways, up and down the street lit by gaslamps every forty paces. It was a standard hazy afternoon, and nothing

Jeshica could see was amiss. Whistler knew better.

"Do you got ANY friends outside?"

"Outside the Ratway?" Her nose wrinkled at the ridiculous questions he asked. The old man's expression indicated he realized the same.

"Look, he's comin. You, Fred, Beratha, and um . . . Kitty. You all are the only ones unattached. He knows, an' he's comin. Now."

Jeshica was already being pushed down a side alley. She couldn't bring herself to plant her heels into the layer of rotting paper and trash to slow them; everything about this was bizarre and frightening, but Whistler was so insistent and she had never known him to be anything but laid back and unconcerned. She had always known how to trust her instincts, and she had learned to trust the instincts of certain others in the Ratway. They knew where the food was, or the deep pockets, or danger. But no danger had ever made her old friend act like this.

"We figgered he'd gone and got himself in trouble with the badges, or dropped from some balcony, or run over. You gotta get gone before he gets here, Jeshica. You gotta."

Finally, she dashed ahead a few paces and turned to look up at Whistler, her arms wrapped around herself and hugging her dull grey jacket close in order to feel her pockets full of all her worldly possessions. The poster crinkled against her ribs. Whistler looked pained, but saw her question before she asked.

"The Ratcatcher, dearheart." His shoulders sagged. "I dunno if it's slavers, or the hack docs, or what, but he comes 'round when he wants and any full grown that ain't attached, he takes. We can't stop him. We try hidin, we try lyin, but they always get found. Some gadget or maybe snitches or—

" He waved his fingerless gloves between them as though clearing away cobwebs. "You gotta git, girl. Go."

"I . . . I can sing on Northside, they got coin to spare an—"

"NO! No singin. Word'd get out; they'd know where yer from. They would know that voice! Know yer unclaimed. Ain't no one to protect ya, ain't no one to miss ya." His chin lifted, pressing his lower lip upward. They both knew it was a lie in the strictest sense. They also both knew he meant "no one that mattered outside the Ratways".

Jeshica took a step back. She'd been too confused and surprised to really feel much else until now. Now, though, she felt tears pricking her eyes. She also felt a whine begin in the back of her throat, but that was easier to fight back than the wetness beginning to pool in her lower lashes. Whistler, too, seemed to realize a line had been crossed. His nimble, wrinkled fingers flexed and then balled into fists at his sides.

"Jeshica, yer sixteen year—"

"Seventeen."

Whistler squinted one eye, but decided there was no time to argue. "Yer old enough, it's dangerous here. I don't want you throwin yer name in the hat and turnin tricks with Yvette, and you ain't settlin fer none of the lads what offered."

Now it was Jeshica's turn to squint. Whistler shrugged.

"Jeshica, you-" he paused. The way the old man's eyes bugged, she feared his heart had given out. His face was pale enough. Then she, too, heard it. Echoing so it was almost impossible to tell the direction, was the sound of barking. An alien sound that took a moment to recognize. Dogs. Dogs were expensive to keep, so no one in the Ratway had even seen one in years. They ate as much as a man, required diligent training, and were often used as symbols of wealth and power in the nicer sections of towns. They also made excellent round-the-clock guards in those nicer sections. In the Ratways, they were horror stories told to children. These monsters were real, however, and were coming quickly.

"Go, girl, go! Who cares where, just go! 'Member ol' Whistler an' GO!"

Jeshica ran. She stumbled over trash and what may have been a body, but each time she thought of turning to look back, she could hear Whistler shouting 'Go!' until one time his voice rose higher, and it didn't sound like words, and the barking quieted or faded into the distance behind her.

She never saw old Whistler, or anyone from the Ratway, or the Ratway itself, ever again.

⚙ ⚙ ⚙

Closer to the wharf, while slipping in and out of foot traffic, Jeshica found another poster. This one was newer, the paper less yellowed, and the image on it was entirely different. The poster for the Melpomene's arrival barely had room for the ship at all. On the sepia-stained paper, the airship seemed to slip through bright clouds that filled the bottom of the image. But standing among the clouds and towering over the ship itself was the true focus of the advertisement. He was immaculately dressed in what seemed to be pressed black pants, a wide belt with an ornate carving over the buckle, and a blousy white shirt with the collar wide open to show his skin almost the same color as his pants. One arm was at his side, hand held in a fist, and the other was lifted up with his palm open and entreating to the sky. His powerful jaw was tucked nearly to his collarbone, mouth open wide in song and his eyes looking off to the same direction of his raised hand.

His name was at the top of the poster, floating huge behind his head: "GERALT". At the bottom was "The Dirigible Melpomene". She had no idea who Geralt was, or how he could be more important than the ship itself, but the change in the advertisements only made her stomach flip with excitement. It meant it was real, and it was today.

And then her stomach growled loudly enough that a well-to-do passerby actually noticed her. He frowned. As her appearance sunk in, and he realized she was far out of her place, the man stopped in the flow of traffic and took a step toward her. Under his stovepipe hat, his carefully manicured brows were low and threatening. He reached a gloved hand under his jacket — and found another hand already there. The man whirled on the small, unlucky boy, and Jeshica saw that the boy was a little better-dressed and a little fuller-faced than she herself was. He had been doing well for himself, right up until this moment. Even as the boy whirled away to escape, the man slipped a hand to his other hip and pulled out an evil-looking glass-bladed dagger. Jeshica did not stay to see the results of the chase, or be implicated as an accomplice. She melted back into the foot traffic and wrapped her arms around her belly to stifle its noises.

She had left the Ratway months ago. She still had nightmares of Whistler yelling after her, his voice echoing down the narrow alleys and blending with the sound of impossibly huge and invisible dogs. Jeshica had remembered her old friend's warning, and had managed to scrounge for food and shelter without ever singing a note. It had not been easy, and she'd learned quickly that her life in the Ratway had been a cozy and sheltered time.

Coin was plentiful, but often just out of reach. Here by the wharf, people were more careful, some even to the point of paranoia. Locks on purses were frequent, and thin wicked glassknives were on the hip of many a gentleman. The idea of having a sliver of that barb broken off and working its way into her belly while her attacker sauntered off convinced of his kill was something she feared more than the badges that seemed to appear and disappear at the edges of the crowd. Best that no one notice her, which is why she had followed Whistler's advice and refused to sing, or barely speak at all.

While she waited for a sign of a purse unguarded or a pocket revealed by a waistcoat, Jeshica listened. She had always been good at listening, but never had it been more crucial than after her evacuation of the Ratways.

". . . left her husband for the landlord and took three month's supply of oil with her. . . ."

". . . children are horrendous. Say they found three birds plucked alive on the balcony!"

". . . had to release the Ratcatcher again. Insufficient evidence, can you believe. . . ."

Jeshica nearly ran into a short, round man as she veered suddenly left in order to find and follow that last trail of conversation. Mumbling her apologies and making sure to keep her head down, she flowed through the quickly moving crowd. The conversation came from a tall slender man walking briskly, nodding his head as though listening to his equally tall female companion as she continued to talk about the local gossip. Jeshica fell in line in their shadow, eyes on their ankles, and took on the demeanor of just another person in the crowd who was bored and irritated and just shy of being in a hurry to get somewhere she did not want to be. It was the best way to keep others from paying attention to you.

". . . say that he was picked up on accident, but you know how those tabloid criers can be," the woman was saying to the ground in front of her. "It takes so long to grow transplants, and there's just such a demand these days. Of course they have to come from somewhere. Why not the scabs?"

"Oh darling, surely—"

"No, it's a tragedy, but necessary of course. The air isn't what it used to be; even though they tell us it's a passing cloud from New York, New Chicago has been sitting under this passing cloud for years."

"It's a very large—"

"Sweetie, sweetie." The woman took the man's arm and pulled herself against him. His head did not lift. "People have a right to live, don't they? You can't take away that option. I just wish they would let the people work their field in the open instead of feeling like they have to lie to us. We know where the scabs go, everyone does. And the city is better for it. Twice!"

Jeshica veered left again, closer to the wharf and the shadow of the balloons hovering over the ships docked there. The conversation was over, and it had made her queasy. She wasn't educated in the proper sense, but even Jeshica understood. Whistler's warning turned out to be truer than she'd thought. What was once a worry about being one day found and sold to slavers and working in some factory or brothel was now a very real fear of being caught and chopped into pieces. The woman had sounded so casual about it, Jeshica didn't even think to doubt. Now she knew she had to get out of New Chicago, and the only ship big enough to have a proper hiding spot was this luxurious behemoth, Melpomene. She would not be the only one, and her plans for how to compete or hide on a ship she had never seen were woefully . . . sparse.

Jeshica followed the crowd beyond the line of docks and into the small marketplace nearby. She recognized a few others who were likely urchins in the mix. They may have been workers on the ships docked at port, but most workers were required to wear a certain standard quality of clothing so as not to embarrass the owner of the ship or frighten off prospective clients. The crew of the ships, however, were always easy to spot. Everything about the crew was designed to draw attention, from their navy-blue uniforms and bright brass buttons to their hard-soled shoes. They clipped and clopped around the market, many with expensive wax keeping their moustaches or chops at a pristine shine. They certainly didn't have time to bother paying attention to any 'scabs' that happened to be nearby. Jeshica, however, noted at least three bright-eyed shoppers who were in no position to be buying anything from the merchants they were bartering with. They cast furtive glances toward the crew as well, watching and waiting, determining their options. She hoped they didn't ruin it for everyone by doing something stupid.

A young man in blue hefted his satchel over his shoulder and clopped his way back in the direction Jeshica had come, along the wharf. She made a show of looking very interested in the imported oranges at the stall next to her. The shopkeeper, beard spilling out over his hefty chest and almost to his round belly, shot her a glance and continued speaking to another visitor. He knew where the money would come from, so there was no reason to even play nice with the scrawny, dirty girl. It was an unspoken agreement. He didn't draw attention to her, and she wouldn't waste his time. They did, however, keep an eye on each other. She'd not be walking off with a free fruit this afternoon. So, empty handed, she followed the young crewman along the docks, weaving her way through the crowd with ease. He boarded the Melpomene without ever knowing he left a shadow on the long boardwalk leading to the deck of the airship. Jeshica tucked in between barrels and rope-laced boxes, preparing for a long wait. In the meantime, she gawked at the monster of a dirigible.

The Melpomene was unlike any other airship that she had ever seen docked at New Chicago; it wasn't built for rugged defense nor for freight. Sky pirates were becoming a thing of the past, and so transport ships were increasingly common and lucrative. Speculators could purchase and deliver large quantities of goods, have them all carried on a single freighter, and be comfortable that their investment would be secure. There was no longer a need to spread shipments over multiple carriers in order to hope for some sort of return when at least half of them survived the journey intact. Those airships were a common enough sight now. But this was no carrier of sugar and produce, this was a luxury ship. Her hull was painted alabaster white, and even the ropes holding the huge balloons to the decking were silver. From this distance, it was impossible to tell if they were actually some sort of silver twine or just coated with some metal spray. Along the side of the boat, on the level of the boardwalk, were lines of old snubnose cannons. Such things were out of date and dangerous, but simply contributed to the effect of stylish elegance and high-fashion with a touch of practical assurance of self-defense.

There was also, at the stern of the great ship, a mass of piping and tubes, all roped off from the rest of the deck. From this angle, Jeshica could see nothing of import about it, but it didn't seem to match anything she had seen on any of the other airships, even those that presented themselves as luxurious travel boats. It didn't have anything to do with the great balloons above, so Jeshica decided it was purely decoration and likely as useful as the wide-mouthed guns along the side. It vaguely reminded her of an old pedal-driven organ.

A barrel was dropped in front of Jeshica's position, and she tucked back further between the canvas-covered boxes. Another was stacked on top of that one, and she found herself, with luck beyond luck, in a nicely shaded alcove all her own. All she needed to do now was wait. Her stomach growled again.

⚙ ⚙ ⚙

Jeshica was awakened by the sound of dogs.

At first, she thought it was part of some nightmare. This was not the far-off baying she'd heard in the Ratways, but even as foreign as the creatures were to her, she'd never mistake their barks and snuffles as anything else so long as she lived. It was dark, and the gaslights cast dancing shadows over her pile of cargo, never quite reaching her with their light. This was no nightmare, and hunger was joined with terror that felt like a rock in her gut.

As the barking stilled, she heard the call of a guard on the gangplank of the great ship Melpomene.

"Who goes there? And what've you got with you?"

"The Ratcatcher, and these are my sons. Who are you?" The voice was quiet and sweet, a low and grandfatherly voice that nevertheless made Jeshica's skin crawl. She couldn't guess how old the voice was, and she didn't dare move to look.

The voice from the ship chuckled, and she heard the clop-clop of boots come down the boardwalk to meet the other voice. "Captain of the Lady Melpomene's guard, at your service. Ratcatcher, aye? I heard you skulk around the inside of the city. What has you and your . . . sons . . . out on the wharf?"

"Hunting rats, obviously. Might you have a few on board?"

"Rats? On the Melpomene? 'Course not." The guard captain scoffed. A dog barked suddenly, loudly, and there was silence for a moment. "We do a full sweep every four hours, above and below deck. Wouldn't be much of a luxury cruise if our passengers had to share space, would it?"

"No, no, I imagine it would not. Are you to leave at dawn, then?" Jeshica heard snuffling sounds coming closer, then fade, then come closer yet.

"A bit after, yes. And could I ask you to keep your . . . sons . . . away from my cargo? Some of my clientele are very sensitive about such things. Not that I have a problem with such animals, of course, but... you understand." The boots clopped past Jeshica's position, back toward the gangplank.

"Of course, Captain," the Ratcatcher fairly purred. "But, should you find anything untoward, do let me know. I will be just here." The guard cleared his throat to speak, but was interrupted. "Just as added security, to ensure no unwanted passengers board your fine vessel."

"Yes, well. Of course. Good night to you." And the hard-soled shoes stepped away onto the ship's decking.

"Good night. . . ."

Jeshica got no more sleep that night, and her stomach was in knots.

⊛ ⊛ ⊛

It was a few hours before dawn when she gradually, oh-so-slowly stretched out her legs. At the far end of the dock, she could still hear the Ratcatcher occasionally speaking softly to the dogs. They would let out a low 'whuff' every now and again. In a slow, smooth movement that felt like it took an hour to accomplish, Jeshica was finally able to peer around the lower barrel toward the ship. It was so close, but also impossibly far away. The gangplank was two meters down from her, away from the invisible menace at the far end, but there was no cover between it and her current haven. Closer was the edge of the boardwalk, and then the side of the ship. From her position, Jeshica was staring down the throat of one of the antique cannons. Around the imposing gun, there was the blackness of the firing room, where a crew could man the weapon and see their target while being nominally protected from return fire. It was, of course, ornately decorated with alabaster filigree that completely undid any menace that the cannon may have had. Lamplight gleamed on the white paint of the side of the ship, almost making it seem golden.

The gangplank was out of the question, now. It was too far, and would only lead directly onto the fully exposed deck. The crew of the ship, even if most were asleep, would have a regular watch. Jeshica tucked back into her hideyhole and began running her fingers over the edges of the boxes that surrounded her. Each was sealed tightly, some with a dozen nails and some with a thick, still-gooey glue. Even the barrels were no help, and seemed sealed to keep their liquid contents from sloshing out in transit.

She was reconsidering the gangplank again when two of the crew loomed over the lip of the Melpomene's deck and stepped down toward the boardwalk. Then they started toward her. Pressing herself as tightly as she could against the cargo, Jeshica made herself into a compact shape of rags and girl, waiting for them to pass by. They did not. First one, and then the second barrel were lifted and hefted up and away from her. She was exposed.

"Don't dawdle, men, we've got a lot of cargo to move before we disemb— what is that there?"

It was the Captain of the Guard, and as Jeshica opened her eyes, she saw him leaning over the railing and pointing a white-gloved finger directly at her. There was no more time. With the urgency of one who was accustomed to running without thinking, she unfolded in a long motion that had her almost horizontal to the wooden planking of the boardwalk. Men shouted on one side of her. On the other side, the dogs started to howl.

Everything was moving so slowly, Jeshica almost felt like she could enjoy the moment. The crew weren't sure which took precedence — the barrels in their arms or the scab dashing toward the ship. The dogs were far away, dragging a large and ominous figure behind them. She felt perfectly safe as she ran the few steps directly at the cannon before her. With a feeling of exaltation, she leapt toward the wide muzzle.

And her stomach turned to rock once more, as Jeshica realized that the ship was not docked directly flush to the boardwalk, but was actually an arm's length from planking to hull. Beneath her, she saw only blackness, but knew that she was high above the clouds without the accustomed stability of the pile to catch her. Before she could scream in terror, the cannon crushed the air from her lungs and she scrabbled with suddenly sweaty palms for purchase along its length. The tiny opening, leading into the gun housing, was her only chance, and she lunged for it, clung with all her strength, and dragged herself inside. Along the wall, she broke the delicate filigree and left a bit of skin and blood behind from her arm. She barely felt the fire of the scrape from wrist to elbow, and kicked off the inside of the wall in order to scamper further into the blackness. Behind her, men were shouting orders, responses, and then they were shouting in fear as the howling dogs and their master finally reached the place where she had just been. Jeshica was on the Melpomene. And now she needed a place to hide. And food.

⊛ ⊛ ⊛

Jeshica was good at hiding. She had been hiding for years, and she was very aware of how useful her slight frame was in such situations. Even as crew stomped up to the room with the cannon and peered inside, she was able to tuck into the corner of the doorframe and wait until they moved off. But with these cramped compartments, she knew they would come back for a more thorough search. She would have to find better accommodations, and quickly. She moved from her shadow, slipped around a corner, and clambered up into a linen cabinet to wait out the next round of hasty inspections. From there, she tucked under a guard's own bunk while he left his cabin empty to search for her elsewhere.

As she moved from spot to spot, she ran her fingertips over the fine details and decorations of the hallways and chambers. There were mosaics on the floor, and relief sculptures on the walls. And the almost gold luster of the pipes was unlike anything she had seen before. There was piping everywhere, some of it labeled, but most of it not. There were also air ducts, but, unlike how they were managed in the places she'd seen in the city, there seemed to be no openings into any of the service rooms, only the square, inconspicuous tunnels that were just out of reach along the ceilings. If the maintenance crew needed fresh air in these lower rooms, it seemed their only option was opening a port hole and hoping for the best.

Abruptly, she stumbled into the kitchen. Three men and a woman, wearing all white and looking quite surprised to see her, stared back for a moment. Then the shouting started. Jeshica dashed to the side, squeezing between brass and steel devices that were never designed to allow people through. A pan was lobbed at her as she snaked her way under a series of tubes. An unsealed opening in the wall was a saving grace, and she tucked her arms to her sides and fell sideways beneath the flooring. Suddenly a whole new world of opportunity dawned on her, and she saw the Melpomene as a stack of latticework through which she would be able to clamber. Her heart soared at the possibility, and the sense of relief that she would not actually be scrambling from search parties for the next few months until she was able to escape into some new city and freedom beyond.

And then someone grabbed her ankle and dragged her across the rough, unfinished boards. In the absolute blackness of the crawlspace, Jeshica couldn't see her attacker, but she knew better than to scream. The smell of him was enough for her to know he was a scab. The breath that washed over her face as he hissed only confirmed it. Somehow, she had not considered the fact that she would run into other stowaways on board. Much less that they'd be violent. . . .

"You little wench, get out of here. This is my spot, and you ain't welcome." He shoved at her, forcing her to cram up against the bulkhead. Then he kicked at her, when she didn't seem to move away quickly enough. And he kept kicking, until even Jeshica's steely demeanor began to crack. She felt the tears in her eyes, and the fire along her arm flamed up as the wound scraped against the rough underside of the floor. The stomping continued overhead as the search went on, and then suddenly stopped. Jeshica shut her eyes tightly, feeling wetness smear down toward her temple.

Light exploded into the cramped crawlspace as a board was ripped up, and then a second. A shadow hovered over the new opening in the floor, and a face appeared for a moment, peering into the darkness. Jeshica and the other stowaway tucked tight against the furthest edges of the crawlspace. Neither of them dared to breathe. The shadow disappeared and the heavy footsteps of the crew moved away as the search continued. And then the floorboards were replaced and stomped back down. Work in the kitchen returned to normal fairly quickly, and muffled voices turned to chuckling jests in a matter of minutes. Silently, the other scab pressed his foot against her and shoved, pushing them further apart and making his intent clear. For a moment, then, both of them were still, listening to the bustle of the kitchen above them and waiting for the other to make a move.

Jeshica shivered in the blackness again and knew that her invincible hiding places were suddenly not perfect safe havens any longer. Wincing at the pain in her arm and the new bruises from the kicks, she crawled inch-by-inch away from the claimed kitchen. She never even felt the gentle lurch as the Melpomene broke free of the wharf and floated gently away from New Chicago as soon as the hazy dawn touched her balloons.

When Jeshica first realized the music she heard wasn't coming from the entertainment gallery beneath the bow of the gondola, she was so hungry that she assumed it was coming from inside her head instead. For three days, she had managed to tiptoe and hide between the security patrols, grabbing what food she could from the tin plates left unattended by the crew. Their hard-soled shoes and regularity with their shifts made it possible, but not easy. Nevertheless, slivers of crust and just enough watered-down-wine to wet her tongue wasn't enough. So it was that, just after the night shift patrol had clopped back to their quarters, Jeshica clutched at her belly in a cleaning supply closet just under the stern. She felt her stomach knot up, then slowly untwist with a gurgle of complaint. One of these times, it would do so just as a blue-garbed crewman was standing nearby, and she would be lost. The threat of being discovered drove Jeshica to desperation.

Waiting five breaths to be sure there were no more footsteps, she stole out into the hallway. Down the hall, around a corner, and into the linen laundry room, Jeshica pressed her foot down on the boards one after the other until she found the one that gave under her weight. Her broken fingernails clutched at the edge that lifted up, and she pried it higher until there was just enough room for her to scrape and scratch her way down under it. As she gripped the edge and pulled it down after her, lying flat on her back, she heard the music again. It sounded like it was coming from the deck above, on the top of the ship itself. It sounded like singing.

Then her stomach growled, and Jeshica pressed herself headfirst along the slats below the walkways. She passed under the laundry, the clothes closet, another cleaning supplies closet, and almost to the guts of the Melpomene itself. The boiler rooms were a place she avoided even exploring. The heat and stench of them were bad enough that she could tell when she was getting close. But there, just on the other side of a bronze-shielded wall, was the larder. Workers were in there now, sorting and preparing food to be brought up to the kitchen for the rich passengers that were enjoying themselves on the proper decks of the airship. Jeshica waited, listening to the sounds of movement, until the workers picked up the last of their bundles and moved out of the room. There was no convenient slat or loose board that would let her get in. So she made one.

Lifting her legs as best she could in the tiny space, Jeshica slammed her heels down onto the very board on which she lay. She didn't listen to see if there were sounds responding to the thud. She brought her heels down again, felt a crunch, and held her breath. One last kick, and the girl dropped from the ceiling into the Melpomene's pantry hold and landed on canvas bags of grain. She knew she didn't have much time. That kind of noise anywhere on the ship would draw attention, but the food for the ship was crucial and the crew would be here if only to ensure something hadn't fallen over.

As quickly as she could find it, Jeshica shoved the lid off of the salted meats barrel. In seconds, her pockets were full of strips of desiccated and crusted flesh from some unknown animal. She couldn't be picky, and she didn't have time to investigate beyond determining which chunks could be easily carried. She stuffed a sliver into her mouth, glanced around, and shoved a different barrel over onto its side. Now for her escape. . . .

Jeshica crouched and eyed the ceiling where she'd put a new hole. It was out of the question to reach it again. But now that she was in the pantry hold, she realized just how secure the room actually was. There seemed to be no exit except the door, and there were already the sounds of approaching crew. Once again, she realized she was backed into a corner, and it was only a small comfort that there was no longer the threat of dogs on board. As the locks turned on the hold's door, Jeshica dashed forward and clung to the wall next to the door's hinges. The door swung open and the two crewmen came in to investigate. Jeshica found herself in the only viable hiding place in the entire room. The relief quickly faded, however, as she realized that her hiding space would disappear the instant they left, and she would again be trapped. Yes, trapped with unlimited food, but also in one of the most frequently searched areas of the ship.

She peered around the edge of the door and watched as the bright blue uniforms moved through the aisles of barrels and boxes, working their way around to the open barrel and its twin that lay on its side. The instant they bent over to lift the wayward container, Jeshica crouched low and slipped around the heavy door and out into the hall. Her heart was already pounding in her ears, making it harder for her to listen for the sound of oncoming footsteps and leaving her relying entirely on seeing any dangers before they saw her. As she came around a corner, it surprised her to see a round porthole at the end of the hall with sunlight streaming through it. Not only had she not realized it was daytime, but the light itself was unusual to her. The light was clear, bright, and unfiltered.

Jeshica was thrown from her awe by an explosion of sound behind her and down the hall, in the storage room she had just left. Shouting and containers being knocked about echoed around the corner, sending her running blind up the small set of stairs toward the port hole. And that's where the short hall ended. She planted her hands on either side of the small window out into the sky, with a momentary thought of crawling out and onto the outside of the hull. Desperation and terror made it hard to breathe. As if to physically fight the urge of opening the circular hole into the clouds, Jeshica turned and leaned back against it, watching down the hall so she could at least see her pursuers before they caught up to her.

That's when she finally took note of the fancy door to her right. It was ornately decorated and obviously led to a passenger's room, despite the fact that most of the passengers were at the other end of the gondola. Though barging into a passenger's room on a luxury liner was almost guaranteed to get her caught, she stood a better chance of finding an empty room than on the outside of the hull. Jeshica was through the door before she'd even realized she was moving. The sound of hard-soled shoes started moving up the hallway toward her and away from the scuffle in the food store.

The door slowly swung behind Jeshica, met its latches, and clicked closed. In the richly furnished room, that small noise sounded loud compared to the silence. She held her breath and stared, as did the tall man who sat on the edge of the great bed in the center of the room. The strip of salt-crusted meat hung from her mouth, and she could feel the tingle in her arm from the barely healed scratch where she first boarded the Melpomene. The man's wide, dark eyes, just slightly blacker than his skin, stared hard at her, then looked up and to the right, and then met her eyes again.

She hesitated, then glanced up and to her left.

There in the wall, just near the ceiling, was a square hole that lead into blackness. That hole was slightly larger than the ones she'd clambered through around the Ratways. It was big enough for her. The air ducts. Jeshica took a step toward the wall, paused to make sure the tall man wasn't going to move toward her, then clambered up onto a chair and plugged her head and shoulders into the vent. There was a knock at the door in the room behind her. Jeshica rolled her shoulders, crawled along with her arms outstretched in front of her, and pulled herself along and into the tiny tunnel. Just as she felt her toes reach the lip and pull inside the shadowy recesses, she could hear the door open. There was no room for her to turn around, so she shut her eyes tightly and listened as hard as she could.

"Are you all right in here, maestro?"

"I am," came a rumbling, resonant voice. It sounded vaguely familiar to Jeshica, but she couldn't understand how. "There was quite the ruckus down the hall. Is anyone hurt?"

The guard at the door chuckled. "No no, nothing like that. We finally caught the stowaway that's been eating our store of fruit right out from under our noses."

The deep voice hmm'ed. "I suppose it will be bread and water for him in the brig, then. I wonder what would drive a—"

"Oh, no, maestro. We don't have room in the hold to keep stowaways, and we're not about to waste foodstores on rewarding those scabs."

"I . . . see." There was stillness behind Jeshica, and the salted meat continued leaching all the moisture from her mouth. "Then what—"

The crewman was obviously waiting for the question, because he interrupted before it was even done. "We threw him overboard. He'll suck cloud for a minute, then. . . ." If the man was expecting a chuckle or approving comment from the tall, dark-skinned man, he apparently did not get one. After an awkward moment of silence, there was the sound of hard-soled shoes exiting the room. "We look forward to hearing your performance this evening, maestro. Sorry to trouble you."

Jeshica began slowly wriggling forward again, now free to explore this new realm of the ship. She realized that she hadn't heard the music in a while.

Hours later, Jeshica had finger-crawled her way through all of the ductwork she could reach, including the forward cabins of the wealthier inhabitants. These she avoided. Too much risk of exposure, and, while she was on board the Melpomene, there was no profit in nicking all the valuables so casually left in plain view. Eventually, she had a good sense of the layout, and felt she could get around safely, though ever-so-slowly. Her vantage points were few, but they were in the more luxurious areas of the aft of the ship. She could see into the bunk of the Captain of the Guard, a few other rooms for which she couldn't determine a purpose, and then the room of the "maestro".

Was he assisting her, or was he simply trying to remain uninvolved? For all Jeshica knew, the imposing man was setting her up for some greater plan in the future. People that were not plotting how to get their next meal had plenty of time to make elaborate plans about other things that Jeshica felt she couldn't even begin to contemplate. And so, to find out more about the mysterious man, she slithered her way through the air ducts back toward the room under the aft deck.

That's when she heard the music again. It sounded far away, but Jeshica could tell it was coming from above her. Something about the melody felt like it vibrated the very walls around her without being loud; it simply matched the very metal of the tubing that roped around the air ducts and snaked through the entirety of the Melpomene's core. It was soothing, and she found herself enjoying it. It was easy to forget how much she loved music, and how much she had apparently missed it. The thought of it brought tears to her eyes just as she pulled herself around the corner leading to the "maestro's" chambers. There was something blocking the vent into the room, and for a moment her heart sank.

Only the sillhouette was visible, outlined in dim light from the room. As she silently worked her way closer, Jeshica was relieved to find that it was a simple cup. Instinctively paranoid, she reached a hand up and dipped a single finger over the lip. Her fingertip came back wet, a little cool, and she sniffed then licked it. It was water. Her mouth cracked from dryness as she licked her lips. The salted meats had been working on preserving her own flesh for hours, and though she'd gotten accustomed to the sensation, the sudden option for relief was almost too much. With very little room to maneuver, Jeshica grabbed at the cup, spilling some of the precious liquid onto the surface of the ventilation shaft in front of her. Thankfully, she was able to move it toward her parched mouth and gradually tilt it to pour over her teeth and tongue.

Too quickly, the water was gone. Jeshica was not too proud to lick a bit of the moisture from the metal. The music continued resonating around her, and it seemed to instill some amount of courage in her, because she had barely glanced around the room before pulling herself out of the vent and flipping her heels over her head to land beside the bed. The "maestro" was not in his chambers, the circular windows looking out the stern of the ship were dark, and there was another glass of water on the bedside table. She gulped that down with none of the care or deliberation of the first one. There were notes, written sheets, on the table as well, but Jeshica only saw one word on the top of each of them. A name.

Geralt.

Geralt was the maestro. And going from the poster she had seen back at the end of her other life, before her torturous exploration of the Melpomene's guts, he was more important than the airship itself. Jeshica couldn't understand. If he was so important, why had he not turned her in immediately? He was so tall, built like a prize-fighter, so it wasn't as though she posed a threat (though she admitted that she could probably do some damage before he simply picked her up and pinned her to a wall). And that cup in the ventilation shaft obviously wasn't something he had been drinking and set aside. She had to find out more, but it wasn't as though she had someone to ask. At least, not directly.

She would wait, and watch.

"But not here," she whispered for her own benefit as she stared at the oh-so-comfortable-looking bed. She was too tired, and falling asleep there would be dangerous. She'd never be able to hear if—

The lock on the door rattled.

Jeshica was across the room and slithering into the vent before the final lock had clicked. She was nearly a meter down the airduct by the time someone entered the room. It took some work, but she got to an area large enough for her to curl up on herself and turn around to work her way back to the dim square of light. She stayed far back and tried to keep her breath shallow and even and as silent as she could.

"And dishes just laying about. What did I tell you?"

"Well you could have said it nicer."

"A scab is a scab, no matter how long they've been trained."

"You sure Geralt was a scab?"

There were now sounds of two of the crew moving about the cabin. They shuffled papers, moved a chair, all as if they were looking for something.

"Absolutely. They put him through all these schools, all sorts of lessons from real singers. He had some raw talent and wound up being better than most of them, so now he's here."

"Guess it could be worse."

"For who?" They both laughed.

"And we just let him run the ship?"

"Let him? You know there were protests, saying he was forced into it?"

"Scabs protesting." A scoff.

"Well, yes, of course. But still."

"And even if he was forced, look at this place. He's living better than us."

"Tell me about it. All right, it's clean. If he's up to

anything, it's not in here. Sun's almost up, let's—" And the door closed. A lock clicked over. And then another lock. All was as it should be in the maestro's room, except for a girl in the ventilation shaft who was even more confused than when she'd first seen the poster of the giant man standing over the Melpomene. She crossed her arms under her chin and rested on her belly, listening to the music until she fell asleep without realizing how tired she'd become. Exhaustion stole over her the same way the sunrise washed golden over the massive dirigible floating above the clouds.

"Why do you do that?"

The voice woke Jeshica up from a dream of falling, and she only just caught herself from jerking in an attempt to flail her arms out. As it was, she held her breath and tried to orient herself. A few feet in front of her, a cup was pushed onto the edge of the ventilation shaft's opening. Her muscles ached as she unfolded her arms and ever-so-slowly managed to push herself further back into the blackness and away from that square of light.

"For moisture, of course." The deep, resonant voice of the maestro, Geralt, replied.

"Moisture in the vents?" The crewman was skeptical.

"No, no," and then came that chuckle. Jeshica liked that chuckle. There was no sarcasm or contempt or hate or that feeling that you were being set up for a trap in that chuckle. It was a chuckle that made you smile without knowing why. "Moisture out of the vents. It's so dry in these cabins, and that would be bad for my voice to have a dry throat, don't you think?"

"Well, of course. Though the other passengers seem to like it dry. . . ."

"Of course, of course. I wouldn't ask you to change anything about how your captain runs his ship. This is just," a pause. "For my own benefit. You don't mind, do you?" There was a smile in that voice.

"No, maestro, just make sure you clean up after yourself. We don't need pests to gather, or mold forming. . . ." Clop, clop, clop and the door closed.

The cabin was still, and then there was the creak as the tall man settled into the only chair in the cabin. Then he spoke to the empty room.

"We certainly don't want any pests gathering," he said, much louder than one would speak if one were just speaking to oneself. "The crew seems very concerned about pests, don't they? I think maybe they hear someone humming in their sleep, sometimes. Probably just a fault in the air ducts, making the wind whistle sometimes. Or maybe the tuning system has some quirks that they weren't altogether made aware of." Again he paused, and there was the sound of water pouring. "That's what I believe it is, anyway. . . ."

Jeshica blushed as realization hit her. He truly was speaking to her, but also for the benefit of anyone also listening to him. Not only did he know about her, he was aware that the crew didn't think any more of him than they would of her. But somehow, his performances were so important that he was like a king on board. A king trapped and inspected and spied on, but a king. She pulled herself slowly forward and peeked around the cup he'd set on the edge of her hideyhole. He was looking right at her with those wide black eyes. Geralt smiled. Jeshica wiggled her fingers at him, then clutched at the cup and let the water soothe her parched mouth and throat again.

"The chef sometimes doesn't treat the pork quite right and leaves it too salty, and it takes a lot of water to make up for that. I like to stay hydrated, so I think I'll keep a bit of extra water here just in case," he rumbled, reaching a hand out to lightly pat his fingers on a large pitcher with a stopper on top. Such a thing could fill "her" cup ten times. Understanding, and realizing that the large man must have seen her stash of salted meats, Jeshica mouthed the words "thank you" from her perch. He smiled for her and nodded.

"It actually reminds me of days back when I was little, when I ate whatever I could get. . . ." And, keeping with the theme of playing at talking to himself, the great Maestro Geralt talked with the girl in the ventilation, and told her of his past.

He'd been born a scab, and, just like a dozen others in his neighborhood, struggled to find his place and to survive. He caught on early that passersby would pause for the musicians in front of the local drinking hole, and so young Geralt practiced singing along with them. Eventually, they enticed him closer with offers of food or coin, until he was a common sight as people would come and go through the dark doors of the pub. He became good enough that those playing would sit back and take a break, letting him gather listeners and bring some change to the hat set in front of their party. Until one day, as he was singing a few paces in front of the group, a man idly bent down and scooped him up and carried him off. From Geralt's recollection, there was no complaint from the other musicians besides maybe a grumble of irritation. But he never saw or heard from them again.

From tutor to class to tutor he was thrown. Sometimes he had people who treated him like parents would, except they were quick to hand him on. Only one face was consistent, and that was the bearded and monocled face of Edwood Clump. Clump owned three ships, and that made him wealthy without anything else needing be said. Two of the ships were freight, and one was passenger. But something else he had was a vision. Edwood was an inventor, and he had invented a steam engine more powerful than any other that he'd seen. Certainly, it ran with coal and old wood stoves boiling water, pushing pistons and gears and all sorts of other mechanics that only the wealthy inventors could understand. Edwood's engine also had a special addition that he bragged about, but held close to his heart, both at the same time. Somehow, the boilers were as basic as they came, but were augmented by a series of tubes topped with glass bulbs that resonated in order to improve the efficiency and effectiveness of the engine one hundred-fold. It was to these bulbs that Edwood would often have Geralt sing. The boy would sing his heart out, following the direction of this strange man who hovered on the edge of his life, before being shooed out of the laboratory and ushered back into the waiting home of his caretakers.

Each time Geralt saw Clump, the man was older and his machine more elaborate. But each time, Geralt simply sang to the bulbs, to either the delight or consternation of the inventor. Until one day, he didn't see Edwood Clump any more.

As Geralt grew, he was paraded in front of larger and larger audiences. Singing was something that was somewhat out of fashion, and difficult for most, but it was a rare treat that many were willing to pay top dollar to enjoy on the rare occasions that it was available. So he would sing to packed restaurants, or dinner cars in passenger airships, or to private parties hosted in tall apartments overlooking a city's edge. Then he was singing into tubes and recording devices so his performances could go places too far for him to travel. His voice was being sold in places he had never been. Eventually, the little scab became a tall, finely trained man, who nevertheless was an anomaly brought from underneath the notice of the people who now stood in line to hear him. And, while they applauded and nodded and bravoed, Geralt was not one of them and never would be. He was refurbished refuse that had found a new place among the elite that would have otherwise disregarded him, or worse.

And then Geralt announced that it had gotten late enough in the morning, and he needed to sleep.

"But," he paused as he slid the covers down over the circular windows and closed off the sun. "But I do hope there is an audience tonight, on deck, as I sing."

Jeshica wriggled silently backwards and into the pitch black belly of the air shaft and once again set her cheek on her wrist to sleep away the daylight hours. She'd seen the intake vents that led to the aft deck. Whatever other audience he had, she'd be ready to listen to that music properly at last.

⊛ ⊗ ⊛

The "performance" was unlike anything Jeshica had heard of before. There was an audience — some of the passengers milled about on the central deck and were served delicacies and bubbling drinks by the Melpomene's crew. She couldn't see how many attended, because the intake vent was facing aft, away from them. Instead, she had a somewhat obstructed view of the bronze tubing and pipes, above which rose the five globes that Geralt had mentioned in his story. And then there was the maestro himself, his thick throat straining the seams of the formal shirt's collar as his voice graced up and down arpeggios and chromatic scales.

Not once did he utter an actual word or tell a story with his song, and Jeshica was entirely entranced.

This, plus the fact that she could not see the audience, meant that it was quite some time before she realized they had all left. At that point, with the clouds only faint ghosts in the distance and the moonlight illuminating the edges of the great balloons above the scene, she rolled onto her back in the vent, folded her hands over her belly, and listened as Geralt drove the ship with his voice. For hours, only briefly broken as he drank a sip of water or took time to eat a small meal, the tall man belted out the magic notes toward the five orbs of glass and the transistors and wires that filled them. They gently hummed in response, almost as though they were acknowledging his coded commands, and soon Jeshica found herself also humming along.

Her breath caught in her throat, suddenly, as a large black shoe stopped just in front of the intake vent. Jeshica was on her back, so the shoe was upside down. It gleamed in the gaslight, and rotated slightly as song carried in the air. Soon the music ended and Geralt took a long drink of water. She heard his voice call out across the deck, booming and confident even without the careful intonation of his song, and so much different from when he spoke "to himself" in his quarters. His was a voice that was used to being heard.

"Is there a problem, night watch? Trouble brewing?"

The shoe rotated again, showing its heel to Jeshica.

"No, no maestro. Just thought I heard something amiss

over here. I thought one of the passengers—" He trailed off, apparently leaving the rest of his statement to a vague gesture that Jeshica couldn't see. The awkward silence continued for a beat until Geralt spoke again.

"Oh, the harmonics? Not everyone can hear them; I'm impressed," he said. "With the resonance of the orbs, and the special design of this ship, it often can sound like another voice entirely. Here, come closer."

The hard-soled black shoes clopped away, toward the recessed stage on which Geralt stood. Now, upside-down, Jeshica could see the crewman standing, one hand holding the other wrist behind his back, in a sort of casual posture of attention. His face caught the light of the nearby lamps each time he nodded at Geralt's explanations.

"The crystal is specifically tuned to capture sound, and the delicate machinery inside is designed to resonate with the proper keys and tones. All of which, in turn, resonates along the other machinery to the engines. It . . . vibrates, but in tune with the music."

"Ah, so, a tuning fork, then? You can plonk the fork and it vibrates accordingly, yes?" With the "plonk", the crewman flicked a finger at a nearby globe. Jeshica could not hear the sound of impact, but Geralt wrinkled his nose before nodding.

"Yes, yes, precisely! Near enough, though with much different results." He placed a large hand on the crystal sphere and caressed it like an apology. "This marvelous contraption is what gives the engine its true power. Without it, why, we'd float along slower than a lazy summer cloud." He smiled and turned to face the crewman properly. "Shall we see if the ship will sing along with me, stronger this time? Perhaps I can train it. You're welcome to stay, if your superiors will allow?" Geralt's eyebrows lifted, invitingly. Almost mischievously, Jeshica thought. The shorter man cleared his throat and, apparently reminded of his duties, clopped away.

Train it? Train me? Jeshica's heart was racing, and she blushed at how excited the idea had suddenly become. She inhaled just as Geralt did, but where she held her breath, the maestro released his in a controlled arpeggio up a major chord to its peak, and then fluttered notes back down. She exhaled in a hiss as she felt the ship respond beneath her. From her vantage point, she could see his hands. One gestured in her direction. Geralt nodded at her, and began the same series of notes up the scale.

Her voice was dull and sounded creaky to her ears, but she opened her mouth and tried to meet his progression of notes, knowing she would never be able to reach his baritone range. Instead, she began higher, thinner, smaller. When he dropped his voice back down the arpeggio, she followed and grew bolder when he smiled.

For hours she followed him up and over the musical commands to the ship. When it finally came time for him to rest and eat at the midpoint of his "shift", Jeshica crawled back through the vents to peek in on the passengers who could sleep through the melodies that powered their vessel.

On the second peek over the rim into an aristocrat's cabin, Jeshica nearly met with disaster. Almost invisible in the dark, her fingertips met with a small object just on the edge of the ventilation shaft's opening. She scrambled and hissed under her breath, catching the delicate cup before it could topple forward ino the room. It was full of water.

⊗ ✹ ⊗

It was near dawn, and Jeshica slept soundly in the intake vent near the aft deck, when sounds began to intrude into her dreams: shouts first, then the stomping of boots and shoes indicating a mix of officers and regular crew. Even occasional passengers wandered up onto deck before being herded back into their cabins and quarters. A general alarm began, then it rose into the klaxon of an all-hands emergency alert. Jeshica found herself questioning what could possibly cause such an illustrious ship to dare upset such expensive and wealthy passengers.

Looking through her small window out into the daylight world, Jeshica could see a square of what was happening. There were blue-suited crew running with some semblance of purpose in front of her. There were the silver ropes tying the great balloons to the deck of the ship, and the ornate railing along the edge. Beyond that were great, billowing clouds. Then something split those clouds, and they pulled back and clung to the armored balloons and patchwork gondola of another airship. Its hull was dotted with vicious-looking spearguns and holes still awaiting repair from other attacks. Some of its victims had apparently fought back; but the fact that this ship was still flying meant that they had lost.

"Sky pirates! Man the guns!" came a shout that Jeshica recognized as the captain of the guard.

The Melpomene's artillery was there, but possibly useless. No one apparently truly expected the few remaining pirates to dare something against such ostentatious mortar guns protruding from the porcelain-white walls. Sadly, the ordnance was outdated, which became all too clear once the pirate ship fully broke from the nearby cloudwall and began firing darts across the deck. The precision gas-propelled bolts of brass-tipped wood bounced and skittered across the pristine planks, except where they found purchase on upright banisters or unlucky crew. In response, the great airship's massive guns boomed once in a volley of explosive shells, then fell silent. Jeshica felt the Melpomene sway under her baloons from the force of the broadside cannons, and she pressed her hands to the walls of her narrow tunnel. Still, she could not bring herself to crawl down into the safety of the belly of the ship. Her eyes were locked on the still-approaching sky pirates. The shells pockmarked the broadside of the patchwork pirate ship, leaving holes that blended in with the ragged metal sheeting and wooden crossbeams of a vessel quite accustomed to damage and hasty repairs. The pirate's approach did not slow at all after the salvo, and it seemed the gunners on the luxury liner realized the uselessness of their own attack. Either that, or the ancient guns simply could not fire again. Jeshica did not know, as she huddled now wide awake just below the carnage of an actual boarding attack.

The pirates were coming for raw material, and needed it as intact as possible. Crossbows and dartguns were brought to bear against the untested crew. In their defense, those manning the mammoth ship did what they could with their flintlock pistols and muskets. Two bodies fell, one after the other, above Jeshica's hideyhole, but she had no idea if they were pirates or officers of the ship. On one hand, she held no love for either group and would fare no better with one or the other. On the other hand, if the pirates pillaged the luxury airship for scrap parts, even if they did not find her tucked away between the decks, they would leave the liner adrift at best. At worst, they would cut the lines and let it drop through the clouds to whatever awaited below. But they would definitely take the engine and leave her adrift—

The engine!

Pushing aside one of the bodies that blocked her view, Jeshica squinted against the sudden light of dawn that poured into her tiny world. Outside was chaos. What she normally saw from this view was yards of clear, dark deck reflecting moon and starlight and the dim gaslights along the rail. Then, beyond that, was the railing around the sunken stage and its dozen globes. Now, however, there were people moving in every direction, occasionally pausing to fire a pistol or crossbow, or their flesh would catch a bolt or bullet and then they would fall to the already blood-streaked planks. And past all the movement and fallen bodies, there was Geralt's place. Slumped against one of the globes, was Geralt.

Jeshica forgot herself. The skinny girl dragged herself out of the vent, over one body, and choked on the smell of gunpowder and blood. She tripped over corpses and men who soon would be corpses on her way to the tower of a man who was leaning on instrumentation so delicate that it seemed it should snap under his weight. No longer was he a voice, or a figure to be spied on from above. He was imposing, still, and his skin was gloriously dark, and Jeshica saw his sweat catch the sun and she realized this was the first time she'd seen the maestro in daylight. But he didn't seem like the maestro now. Now, she knew him as a human and not merely an instrument to move this machine.

"At last we meet," he paused as his breath caught. "Pleasure to meet you, my n-name is Geralt."

A mad giggle threatened to rise in Jeshica's throat. The absolute ridiculousness of the situation, the hopelessness of it all, was too much for her to really grasp. Jeshica caught herself smoothing down her pocketed vest in front of this man she had admired for weeks. Only an instant. Then her eyes were drawn to the wooden bolt protruding from his left side, its bronze tip buried somewhere inside his chest. There was less blood than she expected, seeping through his otherwise immaculate white silk shirt. She inhaled for a scream when his big thumb pressed against her lips and stifled her more by surprise than actually blocking her voice.

Whatever Geralt was going to say next was interrupted by a thunderous explosion just off starboard. Men and debris were thrown across the deck, and at least one figure tumbled and continued off the other side into the bright abyss. The luxury liner rocked and swung from her balloons. The fighting fell to a halt as crew and pirates alike turned and watched the pirate ship, now broken in half and dangling from its own reinforced inflatables, slowly drop out of sight. The clouds lit up from within with yellow-red light as another explosion erupted from the old bombs finally performing the duty they had been built for so many years ago.

Jeshica looked to Geralt, unsure if she should be glad or more afraid at the turn of events, and found him ashenfaced and thin-lipped. His own dark eyes were narrowed and piercing as he looked over her shoulder. She, too, turned, and saw a large man wearing ragged clothes in bright colors stomping across the deck toward them. He kicked the legs of a corpse out of his way as he came around the instrumentation to the short step down into the stage.

"Well, good sirrah," the pirate growled. "It looks like you're our ride home. The Singing Ship, is it? Well, you'll make a fine lullaby for my crew as we feast on the vittles and enjoy this fine ship's payment for the loss of my own."

Geralt shook his head, then raised his hands when the pirate lifted a crossbow to aim at his forehead. "I'm afraid I won't be singing you any—" He gasped and slumped down to sit at the base of the instruments, his long legs slowly unfolding in front of him. Jeshica sank down beside him, helpless and feeling as though she were attached to his side. She felt the blood drain from her face as she saw the spreading crimson stain blossoming from his wound.

The pirate saw it too and muttered some sort of oath under his breath. "We will make a way, if we have to tear your ship's guts apart and rebuild them into a proper machine. Meanwhile, you won't mind if we take your lovely wife as further payment for our troubles?" A three-fingered hand reached for Jeshica and she saw blackness creep in from the sides of her vision. She was going to pass out. And maybe it would be for the best. . . .

"Not my wife," Geralt said, planting his large palm atop Jeshica's mussed hair. "Apprentice. She'll sing you home."

"What?" said Jeshica.

"What?" said the pirate.

Jeshica and the pirate looked from Geralt to each other. The pirate recovered first. "Fine. We've a long way to go. My boys will be getting antsy sitting idle in the sky overlong. Sing, lass." The crossbow was now pointed at her head. Jeshica froze and felt her throat lock up. She couldn't have screamed if she wanted to, much less sing.

"It won't work like that, will it? Tell them—" Geralt choked. His eyes closed. "Tell them your name. Be bold. Like the song."

"J-Jeshica," she said at last. She felt his darkskinned hand under her arm, forcing her to stand. "Jeshica. My name's Jeshica."

"Bold, eh?" The pirate bobbed the sharp point of the crossbow down to her sternum. "Not usually wise to be bold when you're in the crosshairs, lass. . . ."

"Sing," whispered Geralt.

Haltingly, terror in her voice, Jeshica forced a thin trail of sound through her throat toward the nearest of the globes. Its glass casing was scuffed and had a bloody handprint on its surface, but apparently whatever protected it was made of sterner stuff than she realized. Within, she saw tiny gyros rotate slightly, and one object that seemed to be something like a tuning fork give a slight vibration.

"Ahh!" breathed the pirate. "Be bold, he says. So be bold, girl!" Almost as an afterthought, he glanced down at the crossbow still aimed at her ribs and lowered its point to the deck.

Jeshica breathed, and let her voice rise and tremble across a few of the familiar arpeggios she'd sung to accompany Geralt. All of the globes flickered and sparked as their inner workings responded to the song. Another movement caught her eye, and for a moment her song wavered. Geralt's chin now rested on his chest; both his hands were on the deck palms up. His mighty voice was forever gone, but Jeshica was now his apprentice. She would sing for him.

As the girl let the music carry her, mourning her loss and reveling in new freedom, the pirate stomped across the deck away from her. She caught only his first order before he began taking stock of what was left of his men. It would not be easy, whatever came next, but she knew that he did not have much left to work with, and many of the luxury liner's crew had been killed. Survival, now, meant using what was available and making the best of enemies working a single ship. His voice carried back to her under her own.

"No one touches our singer Jeshica. No one threatens her. No one looks at her funny. You slugs want to get home, she's yer queen."

STEAM

SPINNING SECRETS
A STEAMPUNK RETELLING OF RUMPLESTILTSKIN
KATINA FRENCH

The party had barely begun and the band played gaily, but Prudence Miller was hiding behind the curtains already. The rosy color of her cheeks, which matched her ball gown, might've been from exerting herself on the dance floor. At least, it might if she could bear to show her face in public.

On the other side of the heavy damask draperies, she could hear her father's booming voice. He was once again extolling her exaggerated virtues to some poor victim. She wondered if he'd snagged the gentleman she'd seen earlier, leaning on a cane. All the able-bodied men at this little soiree had been fast enough to escape Harold J. Miller, nouveau riche gold miner and world-champion busybody.

"Of course, my dear Prudence isn't just a beauty, you know. Girl of mine, wouldn't do to have her sit around like some useless society belle, right? Right? She's quite an accomplished alchemist. . . ."

Pru shoved a gloved hand into her mouth to stifle a groan. While it was true that she had puttered around a bit with alchemy, she was far from an expert at the subtle art.

"Why, just the other day, she had a tremendous breakthrough! The papers will be beating down my door to interview her any day now, mark my words."

Breakthrough? She'd managed to concoct a simple formulae to take the tarnish off of brass. It was hardly a miracle of science, although she'd been pleased with the results. They had an awful lot of brass in their ostentatious new townhouse. The automaton servants alone required constant polishing.

"And what scientific marvel has your . . . estimable . . . daughter managed to achieve, if I might ask?"

Even from behind the draperies, Pru could hear the barely concealed laughter in the man's voice. She couldn't blame him. It was the best strategy for dealing with Daddy. Force him to either reveal he'd been elaborating the truth, or backpedal his way out of the conversation altogether. Pru hoped he would have the sense and good grace to do the latter. She hoped, but seriously doubted it.

She heard him take a deep puff from one of his disgusting cigars. His voice dropped from its usual blustery volume to a conspiratorial stage whisper.

"I'll have you know, she's solved the Philosopher's Stone."

Pru's face went from beet red to white as a sugar cube.

Oh, Daddy. Forget finding me a husband, you're going to get us laughed out of here!

The Philosopher's Stone was the greatest alchemical puzzle of all time. Only rumors had ever existed of anyone succeeding in its creation. The continual failure of anyone to complete it, after millenia of attempts, resulted in the Great Partnership. Alchemists joined forces with engineers during the Age of Enlightenment. They'd given up and decided to pursue more practical, achievable ends, like long-burning alchemical coal and really excellent brass polish.

Now here was Daddy, at the Rockingford's spring

soiree, attempting to convince some poor bachelor she'd figured out how to turn base metals to gold and live forever! Forget being the laughingstock of Philadelphia society. They'd be lucky if no one had him hauled off to the nearest asylum.

In her shock, she'd failed to follow the rest of the conversation. She could only imagine what the other gentleman said in response to such an outlandish fabrication.

She needed to leave, preferably without being seen. The hosts had left the floor-length window in front of her open a crack to keep the crowded ballroom cool. She pushed it, testing how far it would go. A sigh of relief whooshed out as she opened it onto the lawn. Pru gathered up her rose-pink skirts and squeezed herself through the window, shutting it behind her.

Their steam carriage waited down the street. She could see good old Fred sitting in the driver's seat beneath the gaslamp. His cabman's cap was pulled low and he was leaned back, probably sound asleep.

He's had a much better time at this party than I have.

Pru stepped lightly across the cobbles, until she was out of sight and earshot of the party. Her gossamer wrap had been left behind, probably hung on the back of a chair in her haste to hide from her father after dinner. But it was a mild night, and she didn't mind the brisk air. Back when Papa was just another miner in the Republic of California, it wasn't unheard of for them to sleep beneath the stars on a night like this. But then he'd gotten his big gold strike, and they'd moved east to the Republic of Pennsylvania.

While she enjoyed some aspects of their new life, her father's shameless social climbing and incessant attempts to snag her a high-society husband were not among them. Life felt like an endless masquerade ball, trying to hide her true identity. Four years of tutoring in everything from Latin to deportment meant she didn't fit in back in the Wild West of her childhood. Would she ever truly belong here, either?

As she approached the carriage, Fred's gentle snore stuttered into a cough. He sat upright, shoving the cap back onto his balding pate.

"Hey there, miss! Party over already? Did your father find you a fit husband yet?"

Pru sighed as she opened the carriage door, one foot up on the running board. "No, not yet, Fred. But the party is most certainly over."

❀ ⊛ ❀

Morning light poured through Pru's bedroom window like a mountain stream through a gold-panner's sieve. Her head throbbed.

"Ugh," she moaned. "That's the last time I drink champagne at one of these high-society shindigs."

She'd accepted the fluted glass to be polite, and also thinking it might help settle her nerves. Or possibly calm her embarrassment at Daddy's shenanigans. Instead, it had mostly unsettled her stomach. Now she felt worse than the time she'd snuck some of Old Man Beasley's whiskey back in Redemption Falls.

A shrill scream from downstairs lanced her eardrums, and then ricocheted around inside her aching skull.

Good Lord! Is someone skinning the housekeeper alive?

She tumbled out of the oversized four-poster bed, snatching up her dressing gown and shoving her feet into her slippers. She stomped down the stairs, determined to get to the bottom of the awful caterwauling. She may not have inherited her father's rough-hewn looks, but she got a double dose of his impatience and temper.

The scene that waited for her in the foyer caused her to nearly stumble back up the stairs in surprise.

The front door was closed. Her father was unconscious. He slumped in a heap at the foot of a rococo clock she suspected he'd only bought because he liked saying the word "rococo." A small, fletched dart stuck out just above his shirt collar.

Gearsworth, their automaton butler, leaned against the corner. His kill switch had been thrown.

The housekeeper, Mrs. Honeycutt, was squealing at the top of her lungs in the arched doorway to the dining room. The woman's lung capacity was astounding. Pru wondered if she'd left a promising career in the opera.

Two strange men stood in the middle of the foyer. The shorter, darker one approached Honeycutt. The woman looked terrified, frozen to the spot. A second, taller man with sandy blond hair held what looked like a tiny, ornate crossbow. Each wore a black suit with a crimson rose pinned to the lapel.

The blond man appeared to be reloading the crossbow with a dart that looked suspiciously similar to the one sticking out of Papa's neck.

"I told you, we should have gone with the aerosol formulae. We could have piped it in the chimney and had the whole bunch of them sleeping like the dead before we ever came in the door," the blond man grumbled.

"And then what? Be seen breaking in through the front door? Attempting to climb in a window or bust through the root cellar? Just get that thing loaded and we'll be fine." The shorter man had a slight Spanish accent, like many of the people she'd known in the California republic.

By this time, the shorter man had clapped one black-gloved hand over Honeycutt's mouth. Pru couldn't help but be a bit grateful, since it stopped the screaming. He'd wrapped his other arm around the woman's broad waist as if to restrain her, although she still appeared to be in too much shock to struggle. In fact, she slumped against him, passing out in a dead faint.

He grunted, then slid her carefully to the ground.

"Well. That saves a dart, at least."

At that moment, it dawned on Prudence that she'd prefer to be anywhere, other than on the landing in clear view of two men who'd just incapacitated her father, a mechanical butler, and the sole other human occupant of the house.

She attempted to slip back up the stairs, but it was too late. The movement caught both men's attention. Her eyes widened as the blond man raised the tiny crossbow at her. A small squeak of protest escaped her.

"Good thing, too," he said, as he shot her with the dart. He bolted up the steps towards her. He caught her just before she rolled like a sack of potatoes down the stairs to the parquet.

The last thing she heard was his voice in stern reproach.

"Next time, can we please use the aerosol, Javier?"

❀ ❁ ❀

As a child, Pru had often slept on the hard ground. However, in the few short years since her father's improved circumstances, she'd grown unaccustomed to it. So it was a bit jarring to wake up and find herself on the cold stone floor of a dark room.

She pulled herself up to a sitting position, trying hard to make anything out in the gloom. As she fully woke, a small grey square of dim light resolved itself. A window in a door.

She patted the floor around her, searching for a chair, a bed, anything. The tiny room seemed empty of furnishings. An unidentified scrabbling sound a few feet away caught her attention. That's when she did the only sane and reasonable thing. She screamed like someone had heaped hot coals on her head.

In a few moments, the door flung open. The blond man who'd shot her with the tiny crossbow entered. Pru leapt to her feet, launching herself at the man like a mountain cat, claws out.

"Whoa! Hold on there, Miss Miller." He caught her wrists, stepping back. "I'm sorry, I know this looks terrible, but we mean you no harm. We brought you here for your own protection."

"You dumped me in a prison cell with rats for my own protection?"

She tried to knee him in his nether regions, but he was too fast, twisting out of the way. He grunted as her knee caught his thigh instead. He held her out at arm's length by her wrists, like a particularly distasteful bag of dirty clothes he was carrying to the laundress.

"It's not a prison cell, you ninny, it's a pantry!"

"A what?"

With that, a hand snaked around the corner of the door, flipping a switch. A gaslamp flickered above her, revealing shelves of canned goods.

"A pantry, Miss Miller." A short, rotund man filled the doorway behind her captor. His brushy brown mustache twitched as he surveyed the scene inside. He looked Pru straight in the eye, as if taking the measure of her soul. He cleared his throat.

"Agent Simms, I believe you can release Miss Miller." The blond man let go of her wrists, although he stepped back defensively, as far as he could manage in the cramped space.

"However, I'm afraid he's quite right, ma'am. Unfortunately, while you may certainly leave this pantry, we can't allow you to go home right now."

"But my father!—"

"Mr. Miller is perfectly safe. He should be waking in his own bed as we speak." He leveled a glare at Simms, as if daring him to contradict him. Simms looked sheepishly back at him, dropping his gaze.

"Or at least, waking in his own home. We will send an agent to explain the situation to him in due time. Regrettably, it's a situation he, himself, created."

"What do you mean, he created this situation?" As much as she wanted to leap to her father's defense, she was beginning to have the uneasy feeling this man was telling her the truth. Her father meant well, but he could be foolish when it came to what he saw as securing her future. What had he done? Accidentally betrothed her to a deranged lunatic after she'd left the party?

"Maybe we could discuss it somewhere else? Out here in the kitchen? The parlor, perhaps?" He offered Simms another glare. Somehow, Pru got the impression she wasn't supposed to wake up on the floor of a storeroom.

Now that he mentioned it, she'd be delighted to be out of the pantry, and as far from the man Simms as possible. She offered the mustachioed man her most winning smile.

"That would be wonderful. But, if you don't mind, could I possibly have some clothing, as well?"

She gestured at her dressing gown, nightgown, and thin

bed slippers, attempting to keep the acid out of her tone.

Simms' face reddened.

"We brought some of her things in a valise. They're up in Constance's room."

The shorter, older man hissed out a long sigh of deep disappointment.

"Yes, Miss Miller. You're welcome to get dressed before we talk. I think you're going to want to feel as comfortable as possible to receive the details of this news. I'm afraid your father, quite unintentionally I'm sure, has made you the target of the most dangerous man in the world."

As anxious as she was to hear about the catastrophe her father had caused, Prudence was in no hurry to rejoin her hosts. The upstairs room where she'd found her valise had a washbasin. She'd taken her time freshening up. Simms or Javier had dumped her top drawer's contents into the case and snatched up a few dresses from her wardrobe. She pulled out a dove grey walking dress. It seemed like the most practical thing. After her adventures this morning, practicality trumped fashion.

After brushing her chestnut brown hair and twisting it up into a tight chignon, she donned the pair of boots her abductors had snatched up. She looked in the mirror. At least she no longer looked like she'd been carted off from her bed by bandits in the middle of the night.

She found Simms and the mustachioed man in the parlor. She was shown to an armchair with a polite respect that was clearly attempting to compensate for the rough treatment she'd already received.

"Miss Miller, my name is Myles Grimley. My associate

Agent Cornelius Simms and I work for a . . . well, a clandestine organization, you might say."

"A secret society? Like the Knights Templar?" She'd read about such things in dime novels. A thrill ran up her spine at the idea they really existed.

"Something of the sort, yes. We're called the Boyle Society, formed by the great alchemist Robert Boyle over two centuries ago."

Pru leaned forward, curious at this revelation. Boyle's work with the mechanical genius Robert Hooke sparked the Great Partnership of alchemists and engineers. Their partnership had lead to the invention of alchemical coal, automatons, and practically every convenience modern society enjoyed.

"While Boyle recognized the tremendous potential of merging the Sciences, and applying practical alchemy, he also realized there would be dangers ahead. Let's be frank, Miss Miller. What king, governor or general can regulate or control potions and machinery with unknown capabilities and nearly limitless potential?"

"Doesn't the Alchemist's Guild serve that purpose?"

Grimley nodded, waggling his head a bit.

"In a manner of speaking, yes. They rigorously document all the new formulae and their effects as they're discovered. They declare limits on what formulae and effects are even legal for registered alchemists to attempt, in every part of the world where they have a guild hall. Which constitutes most of the civilized world. But not all alchemists are registered. And not all alchemists are good at following rules."

"Most of them I've met have been more interested in breaking them, frankly. Especially the rules of physics," grumbled Simms.

"Cornelius!" Grimley shot Simms another quelling glance. "Not. Helpful."

He returned his attention to Pru, composing his features into some semblance of a fatherly smile.

"Perhaps it's simplest to think of the Alchemists Guild as the administrative governing body for the practice of alchemy. The Boyle Society is more. . . ."

"The enforcement division?" Pru raised her eyebrows.

"Precisely."

"Mr. Grimley, this is all fascinating, but it doesn't explain why on earth I was abducted at dawn from my home. Or why my father was disabled with a tranquilizer dart like an elephant on safari. If I'm really in grave danger, couldn't your men have simply explained who you were, as you've done?"

"I'm afraid it's a bit more complicated than that, Miss Miller. If you'd come of your own free will, and with your father's blessing, you would not have been able to help us."

"Wait. I thought you were trying to help me?"

"It's both, actually. The man whose attention you've attracted is one of our most troubling adversaries. We've been attempting to capture him for years, with no success. We haven't even uncovered his name. We believe he's building a counter-organization to the Boyle Society. He's been slowly recruiting, or possibly abducting, talented alchemists around the world."

Simms interrupted him again. "Prudence, your father's boasting has convinced a few people that you may have actually solved the Philosopher's Stone. People are speculating your talent, not a stroke of luck, was the source of his gold. If it's even a possibility, you're a prize our enemy can't resist."

"Then why kidnap me? Won't that just confirm for him that I can do what my father said I could? Which, by the way, I most definitely can't."

"We need our enemy to believe you're here against your will, imprisoned for illegal alchemy. It's our belief he'll break in and attempt to turn you to his cause. When he does, we may be able to capture him!"

Pru stood up, propelled out of her seat by righteous outrage. "So what you really mean is, my father's perfidy offered you the perfect opportunity. What you mean is, this is a bear trap and I'm the bait!"

❀ ✸ ❀

Agent Simms leaned against the door frame of the attic bedroom. His blue eyes didn't quite meet her own hazel ones. She sat on the quilted bedcover, pulling her knees up to her chest as best she could in her dress. Some days, she missed the simple, unfussy frocks and pinafores of her childhood.

"For what it may be worth, I was never in favor of this plan."

"Which part did you object to, Agent? I'd imagine breaking and entering is part and parcel of Boyle Society membership. Was it apprehending an innocent person? Dumping her into the cupboard like a sack of flour? Or dragging her into your little secret war against her will?"

"All of it, to be honest." He hung his head, sandy blond hair swinging forward. He really wasn't much older than Pru. "But Grimley concocted the plan of using a counter-agent weeks ago. Once the Head Office got their teeth into the idea, it was only a matter of time and finding the right person."

"Well, I'm so delighted it worked out for you all so quickly."

"Be reasonable, Miss Miller! I apologize for how badly Javier and I bungled things this morning. Things didn't go as planned. The truth is, you may not approve of our methods, but, if we hadn't acted quickly, you'd have fared worse at the hands of our adversary. Your father started this chain of events, at least your part in it. Even if we'd tried to dispel the rumors he started, or come to you and your father in a more conventional manner, the rogue might've taken that as a sign you were an alchemical savant, as well."

"I suppose when your business is spinning secrets and lies, it's hard to know exactly where they'll land, Agent Simms."

"Please, call me Neal. Look Miss Miller, I'm sorry we interrupted your life. I'm sure you were perfectly happy playing the debutante. I'm sure you have suitors lined up for blocks, pining for your return. With any luck, this will be over soon and you can go back to them. We fully intend to return you to your normal life. We're only asking for a little time, in service of the greater good. You have no idea what a threat this man represents."

"Then tell me. Tell me why this man is so awful that it's worth putting my life in danger to rescue the world from his dire machinations."

"Prudence, can you imagine a world not supported by alchemists, but run by them? Where mad scientists are free to conduct any kind of experiment, perform any abomination they can conceive? Where ordinary people are just raw material for them to create monsters or their own personal army? Because that's what he wants. He wants to collect the world's most powerful individuals like a set of dolls, then use them to create a new ruling class based on raw power and the will to use it."

Pru's mind spun for a moment at the implications of such an upheaval. The continental republics had been formed on the idea of individual liberty and rule by the people. The goal Neal Simms suggested for the Society's enemy was worse than a return to the monarchies of Europe. It was either rule by a new breed of despots, who didn't need to raise a willing army or prove a right to succession, or it was total anarchy.

"I see. And you have compelling evidence this is his plan? It seems like madness."

"It is madness, but yes, we're sure. I shouldn't have told you this much. This information is supposed to be confined to Society agents and members of the Alchemists' Guild. But I suppose you are an agent, at least temporarily. We've had a few people get close enough to the enemy's subordinates, pieced together enough clues. We know what he's after. We'd hope you want no part of it."

"Neal, can I ask you another question?"

"You can ask. Whether I can answer depends on the question."

"How did you know my father was lying? How did you know I wasn't a rogue alchemist? How did you know I wasn't already on your enemy's side?"

"We didn't — at least, not for certain. Operatives in our San Francisco headquarters sent confirmation by aetherwire that your father's gold strike was legitimate. The Alchemists' Guild has measures in place to notify them if certain formulae are used or attempted. That's how they find candidates for the registry, when someone creates anything more powerful than a simple apothecary compound.

Nothing had been triggered in Philadelphia. Still, some rogue alchemists, especially wealthy ones, can find ways around those safeguards."

"Is that why you shot me with a dart and locked me in a cupboard? You were afraid I might fling some terrible potion at you?"

She snickered a bit at that thought.

Neal's face reddened. "Certainly not. And if I really thought you were a dangerous mad scientist, the last place on earth I'd tuck you would be a pantry full of possible ingredients. For all I know, you could have built a bomb out of baking soda and vinegar."

Pru wisely refrained from pointing out that one actually could create a weak explosive using those ingredients.

"Then why not just plunk me up here?"

Neal frowned, scratching the back of his head.

"Well, you see, as I mentioned before, we have an office in San Francisco. When Grimley first suggested you as a possible. . . ." He paused, as if searching for the right word. Pru happily supplied him with some possibilities.

"Lunatic bait? Kidnap victim? Unwitting pawn?"

"Asset, I felt it my duty to do a thorough background check. I sent agents out to uncover any information. Let's just say you made an impression on the mining community you left behind. Some of the stories they sent back indicated you were . . . unusually resourceful."

Oh, dear.

Pru's mind leapt back to her carefree youth in the mining camps. She'd had an abundance of energy, an impish sense of humor, and a total lack of supervision. She shuddered to think what stories this man had heard about her adolescent adventures. Especially considering most miners tendency to embellish such tales till they approached folk legend status.

"After reading your dossier, I was a bit concerned that if we left you unattended in a room with a window—"

"I'd shimmy down the drain pipe and disappear?"

"Or up to the roof. Yes."

Well. Yes. Probably.

Pru's righteous indignation had deflated over the course of their conversation. If what Neal said was true, she could understand the Society's willingness to go to extreme measures. She couldn't deny that, if she'd woken up alone in this bedroom instead of the pantry, she most likely would have found a way to escape before they had a chance to talk to her.

She wasn't used to people in her new life assuming she was unusually resourceful. Most of the past few years of her life had been consumed with hiding her resourcefulness, presenting herself as a mostly decorative young lady of quality.

She'd gained new skills and resources, true. It was oddly encouraging to know that the old ones might come in handy, even in civilized Philadelphia.

"All right, then. What do you need me to do?"

"You mean you're willing to help?"

"Are you going to let me go if I don't?"

"Probably not. If we did, you'd only be in more danger. You'd be defenseless against the enemy."

"I don't know about defenseless, but you've convinced me my best course of action is to follow your Mr. Grimsley's plan."

Her breath caught as another possibility occurred to her.

"Do you think your enemy might go after my father?"

"We've already planned for that possibility. My superior officer Javier Hernandez and another agent named Constance Goodwin are secretly guarding him now."

She swung her legs over the side of the bed and bounced into a standing position. Now she had a path forward. No sense wasting time.

"Neither you nor I may like the plan much, Agent Simms. Probably best to just get it over with as fast as we can."

⊕ ⊛ ⊕

On her third day of being locked in the attic laboratory, Pru began to wonder if the Boyle Society was completely full of hot air.

Their plan had been relatively simple. Present the appearance that she'd been apprehended by the Society, and they were demanding she demonstrate her ability to produce the Philosopher's Stone and turn base metal into gold.

Rumors would be circulated where the enemy could not fail to hear of them. He had his own network of spies and informants. It might take him a few days to either send an agent or, in the best possible outcome, arrive himself.

She was beginning to think that their mastermind had outsmarted them, after all. Maybe he'd already discovered she was no genius. Maybe he'd already smelled a trap and was politely declining the cheese.

As the cheese in question, Pru hoped the Society would let her out of it before she rotted up here.

Not that she couldn't have gotten herself out, if she'd really wanted. The attic laboratory was the most secure location in the entire headquarters, possibly not counting the pantry. However, it had only taken her a few hours to find the defenses and figure out a way to get past them.

However it might appear from the outside, she was here of her own free will.

The first day, she'd spent some time puttering around the laboratory. A brass aetherwire receiver spit out card after card of updates from the Alchemists' Guild and the Boyle Society, like a secret newspaper with several short, daily editions.

One detailed several new formulae the Alchemists' Guild had discovered. Or more accurately, formulae some unregistered alchemists had discovered, which the Guild planned to promptly patent, codify and file away for later.

It made for interesting reading. Some girl in St. Louis, no older than Pru, had apparently formulated an antigravity potion and a tracking enchantment in the same week.

Javier, Neal, and, later, the lady agent Constance brought her daily updates about her father. He was worried, but unharmed. As they'd expected, he'd put out several frantic advertisements with rewards offered for her safe return. Anyone who encountered Harold Miller would leave him certain she hadn't left their home willingly, and that he had no idea of her current whereabouts.

Her heart broke at the thought of Daddy worrying over her, but his ignorance was his best insurance.

On the second day, she had an idea. She considered consulting with the Society about it, but, since they'd been in no great rush to tell her their plans, she decided to keep her own counsel about it. She spent most of that day working in the lab, a leather apron tied over her dress and brass safety goggles protecting her eyes.

She might not be an alchemical genius, but she could follow a recipe with the best of them. Two years of study in

"Madame DuBois' Culinary Classes for Young Ladies" had ensured that.

On the third day, she had nodded off in an overstuffed armchair by the attic fireplace. The laboratory looked like a bomb had gone off.

Mme. DuBois could drill her into following a recipe, but not cleaning up the mess.

She found herself awakened before dawn by a most peculiar smell. Like sulfur and cinnamon, as if someone tried to make French toast with rotten eggs.

She looked up to see a very short man leering at her.

His black hair was combed back severely from a peaked forehead. He had an impish grin, circled by a mustache and sharply pointed goatee. Tiny spectacles rested on his long, pointed nose.

"Good morning, my dear." He had a slight accent. Something vaguely European, but beyond that, Pru couldn't say.

She jerked upright, startled by his sudden presence. He put a finger over his lips.

"Ah, ah, ah. Let's not wake your hosts, shall we? Or should I say captors?"

"Who are you?"

The man chuckled quietly. "Many people would like to know my name, my dear. Let's just say I prefer to make sure anyone with that information is someone I can trust. And I don't trust anyone."

"Then why are you here? I assume you didn't materialize in a locked attic to not introduce yourself and then poof yourself back home."

That earned another chuckle.

"I like you, my dear. You have, what do they say? Spirit.

A bit of the rebel about you, yes?"

"Look around. I'm locked in a secret lab, the prisoner of a secret society of bureaucrats. You don't end up in a place like that by following the rules, do you?"

"Ha! I do like you, my dear. And I would like to help you out of your current predicament. I believe we might be able to come to a mutually beneficial arrangement."

"What do you bring to this arrangement?"

"The real Philosopher's Stone, along with the formulae to produce it."

"Really? Why not promise me a magical leprechaun and my own personal unicorn? Besides, I supposedly already have that. It's why I'm here in the first place."

"Come now, Prudence. You and I both know you're no more capable of conjuring the Philosopher's Stone than that footstool in the corner could. But if you could convince the Boyle Society and the Guild of your abilities, we might both get something we want."

"And what would that be?"

"You'd get your liberty. Once you produce the Stone for them, they'll register you in their little book, assign a spy to skulk around after you, and you can be on your merry way."

"What do you want in return?"

"Nothing much. Just a favor."

"You're willing to trade the Philosopher's Stone for a favor?"

"Once you're accepted by the Guild, you'll have the authority to enter any of their guild halls or society headquarters. I find it helpful to have friends in that position. Friends who owe me a favor."

"Won't the discovery of the Stone bring a lot of

attention? It might be hard for you to contact me without their knowledge if I'm mobbed by the press everywhere I turn."

"The 'discovery' of the Stone has happened many times over the years. The press has never heard a word about it. The Guild has made certain of that."

"What do you mean?"

"The Guild already has the formulae. They've had it since Boyle's day. Whenever an alchemist is successful in recreating it, they register the poor fool and then wipe the formulae from his or her mind."

"They do what?"

"They pluck the knowledge from the alchemist's brain, like a gardener plucking a weed from a rose garden. Otherwise, we'd have a cadre of immortal and fabulously wealthy alchemists running around, doing whatever they pleased."

He gave her a wicked grin, as if he thought that was a marvelous idea.

"So you're offering me the formulae, because you know I can't keep it."

"What good would it do you, my dear? You, of all people, hardly need more gold, do you? And who wants to live forever? Where's the fun in that?

"You've attracted the notice of some very powerful, difficult people, my dear Prudence. We both know you could escape this attic any time you want. You haven't, because you know what I know. They'll never stop chasing you. Running will only convince them they were right about you.

"But once they believe they've got you properly leashed, they'll let you go. You'll get your delightfully boring little life back. Aside from having one of their insipid bloodhounds follow you around, which you'll most likely never notice, you'll never cross their minds again."

"What about you? What if I change my mind when the time comes to pay back this favor?"

"Oh, Prudence. I would hope you'd live up to your name, my dear girl. As you said, I've materialized inside my enemy's secret laboratory without triggering a single alarm. Trust me when I say that I am infinitely more powerful and difficult than the people who've captured you."

Pru's mind was reeling from all these accusations and inferences. Was it true? Had the Alchemists' Guild kept their members under control all these years by altering their memories? Stripping them of their greatest achievements?

Then again, considering what Neal had told her, the idea that this man might have an eternity to pursue them forced her to consider the possibility that the Guild was justified.

Each time she thought she had a grip on the world as it really was beneath her suppositions, a new layer was stripped away to reveal more dark secrets.

She composed herself and stood, offering the man a wry smile.

"You make an excellent argument, sir. I believe I'm ready to agree to this deal of yours."

"I'm pleased you're willing to see reason, my dear."

A sound from the stairwell caught Pru's ear. It was a tiny noise, but she knew she was running out of time. The man must have noticed it, too. He glanced at the door, reaching into his greatcoat and stepping away from her.

Impulsively, she leaned forward, wrapping her arms around his neck.

"Then let's seal it with a kiss."

With that, the door to the attic burst open. Simms, Javier,

Constance and Grimsley ran into the room, bearing a variety of sidearms. A stately-looking man with his hand tucked into a large leather bag followed them.

The dark man pulled a glass vial from his coat, flinging it to the attic floor. He shoved Pru away from him. The man leaped into the cloud of sparkling light that rose from it in a shimmering, iridescent column.

And then he was gone.

"Portal potion! I should have known!" The elderly man accompanying the Society agents slammed a fist into his other palm in frustration. The whole company seemed to be arguing with one another.

But Pru wasn't wasting any time listening to them. She ran to the laboratory work table and pulled out a vial of liquid. She dropped something into it.

It began to glow with a golden light.

"What on earth is that child doing?" the elder man exclaimed. He had a British accent, although it sounded very different from any of the English aristocrats Pru had met in society circles.

"Being resourceful!"

With that, she slugged back a drink of the potion before anyone could stop her.

She felt woozy for a few seconds. Then she ran to the attic window, peering through the iron bars out at the city.

"There he is! I knew it!" She practically jumped up and down with excitement. Off in the distance, a few blocks away, she could see a golden glow. It was moving away at a rapid clip, in the direction of the waterfront.

"You'll have to go quickly if you want to catch him!"

"What are you talking about, Prudence?" Neal had run up to the window, and was staring out at it, trying to see what she was talking about.

"I made the tracking formulae. From the Guild reports. I think they called it followfellow or some such nonsense"

"The one that girl in St. Louis invented?" The older man's eyebrows were raised almost to his grey hairline.

"Exactly! I managed to grab a few hairs from the man's head when I reached around his neck—"

"That's what you were doing?" Simms exclaimed.

"So this potion will show us where he's going! My dear, you're a genius!" The elderly man grabbed both her shoulders.

"Well, not really. But that's not important at the moment. If one of your agents drinks the potion, they'll see a glowing trail. I'd hoped he might not be able to send himself very far, and I was right."

She pointed out the window, to the illumination only she could see.

"There's a big bright spot there, two or three blocks away, and I can already see it moving! Hurry, and you can still catch him!"

Constance and Javier drank down the remaining potion, wobbled a moment, and bolted out the door together.

"I can't believe they just drank that. They hardly even know me."

Grimsley walked up to the window, glaring out it as if he could see the potion's beacon by sheer force of will.

"Well, for one thing, they're damn fools who jump first and then check the water depth. For another thing, this is the closest we've gotten to this blighter in a decade."

He turned and regarded Pru for a moment. "As for you, this wasn't part of my plan—"

"Are you seriously going to criticize me, Mr. Grimsley?

I saved your plan, which would have been a total failure without my contribution."

"You're absolutely right. Although, to be fair, he shouldn't have been able to create a portal out of here. We'd already prepared for that. It will take the Guild's finest minds weeks to determine how he countered our backup enchantment."

He turned and joined the older man as he headed back down the stairwell, much more slowly than Constance and Javier.

He paused at the door, and turned back to Pru and Agent Simms, who was still standing next to her.

"I was going to say, we could use someone with your gift for extemporizing in the Society. I'm good at strategy, but we need field agents who can improvise when the circumstances require it. I think you'd make an excellent agent, Miss Miller. With a little training, of course."

He pulled a pipe out of his pocket.

"Robert, if you don't mind terribly?" He lifted the bowl of the pipe in the direction of the older man.

"Not at all, Myles." The man reached into his bag, and sprinkled something into the pipe. A blue flame six inches high spurted out, and then quickly disappeared, leaving a trail of smoke pouring out in its place. Grimsley puffed on the pipe and offered Pru one last appraising look.

"Something to consider, Miss Miller. Unless you'd prefer to return to the high society marriage market?"

⊛ ⊛ ⊛

A week later, Prudence Miller was enjoying a delicious luncheon of lobster bisque at one of Philadelphia's finest restaurants. Society matrons would have been scandalized if she had been seen sitting alone with an attractive young man with sandy blond hair.

Fortunately, what they saw was what looked like a prim lady's maid.

"I can't believe I agreed to this," Simms grumbled.

"Why? It's not like you're actually wearing a dress and bonnet. It's just an illusion."

"We could've just made me invisible. It's actually a simpler formulae."

"And then I'd look like I was talking to myself. Which is not much better than being caught alone with a man."

He grunted, and leaned back in his chair in a very unladylike pose. An older woman two tables over gawked at him. He wiggled his fingers at her in a saucy wave.

"So they've definitely lost him, then?" Pru sighed in disappointment.

"Yes." Simms gritted his teeth. "He had an airship waiting, and then a series of portals. The trail's gone cold."

"So it was all for nothing." Pru leaned her cheek dejectedly on her hand. She'd been really hoping to have been responsible for the capture of the world's most formidable criminal, before she was even an official agent of the Boyle Society.

"Hardly. We nearly caught him. We were on his trail so fast, we managed to get a name. It may be an alias, but it's more than we've ever had to go on before. The man has been a complete vapor, a phantom, for decades."

"What was the name?"

"Something ridiculous. Valentine Myrmidon."

"So I got you his name."

"You got a name. Probably not the real one. But if it's a name he's used at all, it'll be helpful. The Guild can create some pretty amazing deductive formulae with just a name."

"Well, that's something, I guess."

"So, have you decided whether to take Grimsley up on his offer?"

Pru took a long slurp from her soup bowl. This whole affair had turned her world upside down, but, in less than a week, everything was back to normal. Not that normal was all that spectacular.

Her father still wanted to marry her off to some blue-blood.

The blue-bloods still wanted her money while looking down their patrician noses at her.

The Society and the Guild, with all their secrets, made her father's meddling look like a harmless parlor game. But they offered her something she'd never believed possible: a role in life more influential than a rich man's wife or daughter. They offered her a chance to make her own mark on the world.

If she joined the Society, she could use the skills she'd gained in both her old life and her new one for the common good.

It would be difficult, keeping a secret life hidden from her father. She'd have to continue to outsmart his plans to marry her off. But it was worth a try.

"I have. I'd like to accept. What do you need me to do next?"

Simms smiled, and slipped an envelope from inside the black coat that only she could see, since everyone else saw an old maid in a dowdy day gown.

"I thought you'd say that. It just so happens that we have a little mission, and you might be the perfect person for it. . . ."

THE END

THE CASE OF DAREBIN SHIRE

JAMES WILLIAM PEERCY

Two clicks. The metal eyelids clapped together as the thin gold iris focused on its prey. The steam in its belly built pressure. The pistons which drove its legs prepared to leap. The hollow tube wings extended for the glide.

Its sharpened claws screeched against the train's roof top as the creature launched into the air. Hot steam shot through its nostrils with a whistle few could forget. It was the cry of the brass wyvern, and it was after Aaron. The ten year old boy knew it by sound. It stalked the streets of the city at night before the sea's mist came in.

Aaron leaped from the walkway. Striking the cobblestone road with his leather-soled shoes, he slid to the left. Where his shoulders had been a moment before, metal claws clicked together as they gripped the empty air.

Heart beating wildly, Aaron bolted down the side of the building. His breath came out as small puffs disappearing into the cold air. The dark image of the boy raced through the cross streets. He counted them one at a time; he did not want to miss his turn.

It was above him; he could sense its gaze as the wyvern circled in the heavens. For the second time, its sharp eyes caught his movement and dove.

The stairs were before Aaron. With his left hand, he grabbed the railing and thrust himself at a ninety degree angle. In rage, the brass wyvern swooped by, calling into the night. Aaron's feet didn't stop till after he passed through a wooden door. As he reached the room below, he slammed the door behind him.

In the past as he did this, his older sister would glare at him and say, "What the Dickens are you doing out there? You know the mist has to rise first!" Eyes wide and lungs heaving, Aaron looked over to where his sister, Ada, used to sit. He could imagine his response to her even now. "Trying to get a jump on the other scavengers. Someone's been picking the dust-bins clean."

His sister always sat at the table. One table leg was broken, so a box had been placed to hold it up. Behind her would be a fire in the small hearth, burning a scavenged cedar log. She liked cedar; it would pop and crackle, sending sparks to land on the hard-packed, dirt floor. She always said it gave the place a feeling of home.

He was living in an abandoned room beneath a house that was for sale. The odds of anyone buying the house were virtually nonexistent. People were leaving Darebin Shire, not moving into it. The brass wyverns were seeing to that.

Nodding toward the pot hanging over the fireplace, his sister would sigh. "The gruel is hot. If the mist rises tonight, I'll see what I can find."

Aaron's face would always flush. "No, that's my job. You know what will happen if they find you."

Ada's eyes always narrowed for a fight, but then they would soften. "I know. It's the reason mother and father are gone."

It was getting too painful to come here. She hadn't listened, and now she was gone, too. The room was silent and cold; no fire burned to warm it. The pot over the fireplace was empty, and, because he had been chased by the brass wyvern, odds were there would be no food tonight.

In one corner, there were two blankets and a pocket watch; they were the last items that had come from his home. He picked up the pocket watch; it reminded him of his father and the times they had worked at fixing clocks together. If something happened and he couldn't make it back, he didn't want to lose this. He placed it in his pocket.

His stomach gurgled in complaint, but there nothing he could do. Unless the mist rose, finding food was near impossible.

Grabbing one of the blankets, he rolled it up and went back to the exit. His fingers pulled the wooden door open, enough so he could peer into the sky. The moon was rising. Full moons at night were the worst. The darker the night and the higher the mist, the less the wyverns would see you.

With silent feet on the stairs, Aaron crept to the top one by one. If he could find a place to hide up here, it would be easier to know if the mist rose.

Across the way was a dust-bin; he had never seen it there before. Someone must have moved into the home, but who would dare come to Darebin?

It was worth the chance. If he could get there without being seen by the wyvern, not only could he watch, but he might find food. Despite the glow of the moonlight reflecting from the cobblestones, he set his jaw and raced across.

The screech was back. The brass wyvern knew he

was there. With a whistle of expectancy, it dove directly for him. Aaron leaped forward, diving into the shadow, but the metal claws were outstretched, ready to strike.

The backdoor of the house jerked in, and a man holding a crossbow with an extra-thick shaft took careful aim. "Stay down, boy!" As he touched the trigger, a tiny burst of light leaped from the end of the shaft, shooting steam. Aaron's eyes widened. The bolt burned brightly as it soared into the air.

The creature's eyes narrowed. Collapsing one wing, it spun to the right, shifted its position, and brought its wing back out to flap its way toward the heavens.

"Drat!" The man spun around. "Hopefully, that arrow hits the water!" Stepping inside, he slammed the door.

Aaron let his head drop back and stared up at the sky. Whatever the man had done to the wyvern, it certainly did not like it. The dust-bin was behind him. If he stayed quiet, he might be able to search it before he left.

The door jerked open again, and this time the man held an oil lamp. The lamp cast an orange glow, washing away the shadows. "Well, are you coming in, or do you like playing hide and seek with the wyvern?" Before Aaron could respond, the man stepped out, grabbed him by one arm, and pulled him into the house.

The moment the man released his arm, Aaron backed up to the nearest wall and stared around the room. Various contraptions sat on tables and chairs, leaving only one or two stools to sit on. He understood the parts they were made of, though not necessarily their purpose. They were gears, levers, and other small pieces he had helped his father use when putting together clocks. The smell of potato soup cooking over the hearth wafted toward him;

his stomach growled.

The door slammed shut. Aaron spotted the man's crossbow in one of the few empty spots on the table. The man glanced at the boy. "Relax. I'm not here to hurt you. I'm here to help the town."

Curiosity overcame Aaron's fear. "Who are you?"

"Dr. Orville Seth Zebulon at your service, but you can call me Oz." He watched Aaron's eyes dart toward the hearth. "Grab a bowl on the counter, if you're hungry. I don't go on formalities." Turning back, Oz picked up a bolt and started reloading the crossbow.

There were five or six bowls on the counter, but only two were clean. Though on the street he would not have been picky, he chose a clean one and headed to the hearth.

Picking up the ladle, he filled the bowl almost to the top. The hot, creamy smell struck his nose and made his stomach gurgle more. Without waiting, he placed it to his lips and tasted it. It was hot, but he was too hungry to wait any longer.

"How long have you been on your own, boy? When did they leave you?"

Aaron stopped and forced his voice to be steady. "Why do think I'm on my own?"

Oz chuckled. "For one, you're trying to find scraps when the wyvern is out; this shows no street sense. For two, you selected a clean bowl. That means you recently took to the streets. Kids that grow up on these streets don't really care."

Aaron looked at the soup and considered the man's questions. It was a fair trade. "My parents didn't leave me. They were taken one season ago. My sister was taken a week back."

Oz gave a nod. "Do you have a name?"

The abruptness threw Aaron. "A-Aaron."

"Well Aaron, I've good news for you. I need someone to help hunt these wyverns, and you need a place to stay. If you help me, I'll help you. Deal?"

The warm hearth and soup tugged at him, but he didn't quite trust the man. "I — I don't know."

"Fair enough." Hefting the crossbow up on his shoulder, Oz turned toward the door. "If you're still here when I get back, I'll take that as a yes." Throwing the door open, he stepped out into the night. "Oh," he looked back in quickly, "just to let you know. I believe in trust, but if you take anything and run, I will find you."

Aaron's eyes widened; he had thought just that. If he decided to leave, he could trade what he took for food. How had the man read his mind? Maybe there was truth behind what the man was saying; he could really use Aaron's help.

He swallowed quickly. The soup warmed him from the cold outside. He considered eating a second bowl, but his eyes kept darting to the backdoor. Oz was out there hunting the wyvern. It was the first time he had seen anyone try. Setting the bowl beside the hearth, he turned and followed after, closing the backdoor behind him.

It was two cross streets before he heard the whistles. Two wyverns were circling overhead, and a third was dropping from the sky. A cross bolt launched, scoring directly into the body. Sparks flew as yellow flame leaped from the wounded wyvern's side.

The bolt exploded, and chunks of metal shot off in all directions. Pistons and gears dropped toward the earth, bouncing off buildings and coming to rest on the cobblestone road.

Lights in the houses began to glow. Shutters moved back as windows were opened. People looked out the windows and stared in wonder at what was going on. The two circling wyverns headed off toward a building at the town's edge. Oz hopped up on top of a large box and studied the sky around them. The wyverns were nowhere to be seen.

"They're smart," Oz gave a nod, "and don't you forget it. The man who created them lives in that tower."

Aaron's eyes looked across the inlet where ships would come in the day. A tall, black clock tower stood above the other buildings. Gas lights flickered, casting a golden hue. The tower was attached to a smaller two-story building just at the edge of Darebin. Oz's intent was clear, but Aaron had to voice it. "You're going there?"

Jumping from the box, Oz landed on the cobblestone road. "Yes, and I'm going tonight. By morning, I want those wyverns dead."

Aaron stared at the tower. It was the wyverns who had taken his parents and sister. The words came out before he could stop them. "I want to go, too."

"It'll be dangerous, more so than running from one in flight. Are you sure you're up to this? There could be anything in that tower."

"I am."

Oz gave a grin. "Well then, let's go get ready."

The return to Oz's house was quick, and within minutes they were ready. Oz placed a belt around his waist and slipped on a brown, full-length coat. He picked up the crossbow and dropped a quiver filled with his special bolts on his back.

On his belt were round globes decorated in alchemist

runes. There was a metal button at the top of each. He handed a belt to Aaron. Aaron put it on.

"These are fire globes." He pulled one from his belt and showed it Aaron. "You press here," he pointed to the button on top but was careful not to touch it, "and then throw it like this." Without releasing it, he demonstrated. "The button cracks the glass in the containers. You have about three to five seconds before the two elements coalesce." A grin lit his face. "It's a little gift from an alchemist," his hand snapped it back to his belt, "and great in pinch."

Aaron touched one of the globes. He had never seen anything like it. The belt was heavy, but not awkwardly so. When he looked up, Oz held out a smaller crossbow and quiver.

"You think you can handle this?"

Aaron stared at the crossbow. It was easy enough to see how it worked. The string was brought back by a lever, and a trigger released the string. There was a half circle cut out all the way down the crossbow's shank where the bolt fit in and traveled as it was shot. A small slot existed in the shank with a piece of metal sticking up. When the arrow was loaded, a second slot on the arrow lined up with the slot on the shank. This allowed the piece of metal to strike a spark. The spark started the process which would help launch the bolt using compressed steam power. Aaron dropped the quiver over his shoulder, pulled a bolt out, and loaded it. Hefting the crossbow just like Oz, he waited.

"And a quick study, too," Oz grinned. "Come on."

They left through the backdoor. By now, the moon was high. It reflected off the roof tops of Darebin and cast an ominous glow on the dark, clock tower.

Aaron studied the hands of the clock as they walked; it

was almost midnight. The mist was rising off the water, billowing in toward the town. By the time they reached the walking bridge at the far end, the mist had arrived.

Their feet sounded as they walked the wooden bridge with its waist-high handrails. The supports for the handrails were designed as swallows dipping and turning in a playful sky dance. It was the bird that had given the town its name. However, with the coming of the wyvern, even the birds had left Darebin Shire. Anything that moved was at risk. Anything that moved could be taken.

The clock tower loomed taller as they approached. As if pushed forward by an unseen hand, the mist swallowed the land behind them. This was the time the scavengers came out to search the dust-bins. It was the time when average people stayed safe in their homes.

Stepping from a side street, Oz stopped; in front of them stood the house that attached to the clock tower. Bringing his crossbow from his shoulder, he checked the fit of the bolt and the string. Aaron did the same. The gate groaned as they passed through; Aaron was sure that someone inside should have heard it, but nothing stirred. Walking down the path to the entrance, they both stopped at the single, short step.

Oz motioned toward the door. "Shall we?"

As Aaron nodded, Oz pulled some small tools from his pocket, stuck them in the keyhole, and began to move them up and down. The lock clicked. Putting the tools away, he reached forward and turned the handle; the door swung back.

The gas lamps were off in the living area. A single lamp burned on the stairs. A growl issued from somewhere at their right as the sound of gears kicked into motion. Two red eyes glowed to life in the darkness as the metal eyelids opened. With slow grace, the mechanical dog stepped into the moonlight that shone through the open door.

Man and boy backed up. The mechanical mouth dropped, showing massive jaws with sharp iron teeth. Steam came from its nostrils, not unlike the brass wyvern. Aaron saw the pattern; the same man who had built the wyvern had also built the dog.

Oz kept his crossbow level. "Good boy, good dog."

Metal scraped metal as the mechanical dog snapped its jaws. Its eyes moved from the boy to the man, swinging its head back and forth.

"Aaron, the hall to the tower is behind us. On my count of three, we need to run that direction. Ready?"

Aaron nodded with wide eyes as he watched the dog's head move.

Reaching slowly to his belt, Oz removed one of the fire globes. "One." The sound of cracking glass met their ears as he pressed down the button. "Two." With a slow upward pitch, he tossed it toward the dog. The iron jaws snapped again, catching the globe in flight. "Three."

Oz turned, saw Aaron was still staring, grabbed the boy's arm, and pulled. Snapping from the trance, Aaron began to run.

The head of the mechanical dog exploded; parts and pieces shot in different directions. Aaron could feel the pelting on his back. The dog's body shifted left and right, no longer able to see or hear them, but it did not stop. Knowing the last direction they had gone, the headless dog gave chase.

The hall ended at a wall. There was a narrow door on the left and red carpeted stairs on the right. They leaped toward the stairs, grabbed the ornate railing, and raced up.

The dog rammed into the wall. The neck jammed into its stomach. Bouncing back, its body began to wobble.

Oz increased his pace. "Up! Quickly!"

They moved past the first floor platform and onto the second floor. Aaron had expected to hear an explosion, but nothing came from below.

Thick oak doors stood out on all sides. In the center of the doors were small iron covers, about six inches by six inches, latched shut. Oz caught Aaron's glance as they headed up the stairs to the third floor. "Cells. Apparently the master of the house likes to keep prisoners."

The third floor was the same; it contained more doors with covers. However, the third floor stairs lost the carpet and became bare wood. The ornate railing was gone, replaced by a plain, iron rail. Without the carpet, their footsteps were louder as they headed toward the fourth floor.

A door was at the top of the stairs. They could hear noise behind it. Oz checked the handle and found it unlocked. With a twist, the door swung in.

Huge gears looked down upon them. A trail of wooden planks led around the side. The boards creaked as they slowed their pace. At last, it opened to a work area.

The work area faced the back of the clock. The glowing of the gas lamps lit the inside of the work area, giving the clock its outer glow. Tables with gears, screws, and shafts were everywhere. On one, pistons were assembled. On another, hollow tubes were being combined with a silk material, creating wings.

There were men at the tables. Thick iron bracelets decorated their ankles and were attached to the wooden floor. A curly haired man with brown hair caught Aaron's attention. "Father?"

The man jumped and gradually turned toward the sound. A look of wonder crossed his face. "Aaron?" Tears welled up in his eyes. "My son! How did you get here?"

Aaron rushed toward him as Oz stepped back out of sight. "Father!"

A surly voice called from the dimmer parts of the room. "Not so fast, boy." Stepping forward from the shadows, the man wore a black coat, a red silk vest, and a black top hat. A fob was attached to his vest, leading into a pocket. In one hand was a gold-topped walking stick in the shape of a wyvern's head; the wyvern's eyes glowed ruby red in the light. The man's eyes narrowed at Aaron. "You don't belong here, boy, unless you've come to work."

Aaron turned as his face flushed. "You stole my father and mother. You took my sister!"

"Sister?" The man considered, gazing up unconcerned as the crossbow waved in his direction. "Yes, I do believe a new maid was brought in," the man's eyes dropped and narrowed at the boy, "but what concern of that is yours?"

"Let them go!"

A grin spread across the man's face. "And why should I do that, when I control these?" He snapped his fingers; two brass wyverns stepped out on his left and right. Their eyes centered on Aaron. Aaron felt the weight of the crossbow in his hands. The man studied him as the gears of the clock above his head turned. "So, you're the one killing my creations. One crossbow against two wyverns? Shall we see who wins?" He caught Aaron's father's eyes. "Get him."

Aaron's father leaped up, the chair falling to the wooden floor with a loud clatter. "No!" He fought to reach his son, but the chains held him back. "Aaron!"

A maniacal fire danced in the man's eyes. "You see, Aaron, my wyverns have tried to catch you several times, and I intended to use your skills here. I have been secretly bringing in the best clocksmiths to assemble my creations. With them, I will not only conquer Darebin Shire, but will soon take over the world!"

When the man tapped his walking stick against the floor, the wyverns advanced. It was in their eyes; they were slowly savoring the moment they would tear Aaron limb from limb.

In a very calm voice, the man continued, "You have killed one of my creations. For that, the punishment is death."

The wyvern's wings pounded the air, lifting to prepare for a dive. The huge clock gears shifted, rotating the clock's big hand.

Oz's voice bellowed out as he stepped into view, took aim, and fired. "Aaron, now!"

Aaron dropped to one knee, steadied the crossbow, and pulled the trigger. Nothing happened.

One of the wyverns burst into a shower of light. Smoke and steam shot out of its side as it plummeted to the floor. Oz reached back for a second bolt.

Aaron turned his crossbow over, keeping the bolt from falling loose. The trigger was jammed, and there was no time to find out why. He sat back, held the bolt with his knees, and used his thumbs to force the string up.

The bolt launched with a shower of steam and sparks, plowing into the breast of the wyvern. The eyes of the wyvern opened in surprise as it buckled back and then tumbled forward.

Aaron rolled to the right as the wyvern slammed into the wooden floor. The desks shook; assembly pieces jumped.

The man with the walking stick raved. "What the blazes? There are two of you?"

Oz leveled his newly loaded crossbow at the man. "I am Dr. Orville Seth Zebulon, and you sir, are my prisoner."

The man raised an eyebrow. "Indeed? We shall see about that." Raising his walking stick at Aaron, he tapped one of the red eyes. A white-hot flame shot out from the end.

Oz slung the quiver from off his back, jumped forward in front of the flame, and blocked the fire from Aaron. He turned his back toward the man and extended both sides of his coat. The licking tongues of fire surged around him, changing from white to orange. The outer skin of his jacket burnt away revealing strange shimmering material.

Spinning around, the man fled back into the shadows.

Oz, red-faced and sweating, quickly took off his coat and tossed it to the floor. He shook his fingers from the heat. "It's not quite perfected yet, but it works." He grabbed the quiver from the floor, dropped it over his head, snatched up the crossbow, and raced after the fleeing man.

Aaron grabbed his own. As he pulled the lever back to prepare the string, a tiny gear fell out. It must have happened when the mechanical dog lost his head.

"Aaron," his father's face was pale, "where are you going?"

"I've got to help Oz!" The trail they had taken was obvious. A pole passed through a square hole in the floor. It dropped into the darkness. Securing the crossbow, Aaron grabbed the pole and slid down.

His eyes adjusted as his feet touched the bottom. A door had been flung open to his left, and moonbeams shone into the room. He sprinted forward toward the light, emerging in a garden.

They were everywhere, hundreds of wyverns waiting to be awakened. A small metal panel on the belly of one swung back and forth in the wind.

❀ ✿ ❀

"He uses this," Oz held up a small square block, "to power them. It creates the steam which drives the pistons. I shall have to study this."

A scream came from the other side of the garden. Both rushed toward it and found a shattered glass door leading into a kitchen. A brass wyvern stood waiting over the body of an unconscious girl; it was Aaron's sister. Aaron raised the crossbow.

Oz's hand forced the crossbow down. "Wait. It's too close. She might get hurt."

The wyvern turned its head toward them. There was a gleam in its eye. Its right claw hovered over the girl.

Shaking his head, Oz glanced toward the other part of the house. "This is a distraction. Otherwise, it would have already killed her." Putting a finger to his lips, he pointed for Aaron to stay where he was.

With quiet steps, Oz made his way to a study with dual doors. Only one of the doors was open.

At the back of the study was the man they were chasing. He was dropping papers in satchel.

Oz stepped into the room and leveled the crossbow. "It's over." Cautiously, he walked toward the man. "No more games and no more running."

Startled, the man looked up, but a grin spread across his face. On one shoulder, he placed the satchel. "I agree."

The window shattered behind him as two claws struck the glass. Oz threw up his arm to protect his eyes, dropping his crossbow. His hands swept forward as he attempted to grab the man, but the vest made his fingers slip, and he caught one of the vest pockets. It ripped.

⊛ ⊗ ⊛

With a blaze of speed, the wyvern guarding Aaron's sister swung toward the study door and rushed to get through. It knocked the closed door from its hinges and sent it bouncing into the far wall.

Aaron raced forward with crossbow ready but did not fire. The creature was too close to Oz.

Oz threw himself to the side as they both watched the wyvern leap into the air. It soared toward the man with the satchel, grabbed him by the shoulders, and passed through the window.

The wyvern began to rise; Aaron shot his crossbow. The flying creature swooped to the right, avoided the bolt, and began to climb again.

"Farewell, Dr. Orville Seth Zebulon. Till we meet again!" The wyvern and the man grew smaller and smaller until they vanished from sight.

The room went silent. Falling glass bounced off the floor as Oz slowly rose to his feet. A grin spread across his face. He clapped Aaron on the shoulder. "You've done well, boy."

Aaron's face fell. "But he got away."

Opening his right hand, Oz revealed a pocket watch. On the one side were the engraved letters BJC. "No, the man hasn't." He looked up at the sky. "We will find him."

The voice of his sister, Ada, caught Aaron's attention. "Aaron!"

As he turned, she ran toward him and threw her arms around him.

"You're safe!"

He inhaled and made his voice deeper. "Of course I am. I can look out for myself."

"I know you can," she mussed his hair, and her face brightened. "We're all here: father, mother, and the others. The wyverns didn't kill us; they captured us."

"I know," he threw a look at Oz, "and we're going to catch the man that made them."

THREE MEN IN A BLIMP,
TO SAY NOTHING OF THE AUTOMATON
MARIAN ALLEN

There was this chap named Jay and two other chaps whose names I forget, and they took their dog with them and went a bit of a way up the Thames in a rowboat, and the chap named Jay wrote about it, and everybody in England went mad over it, and everybody who could scrape up two friends and a dog tried the same thing.

So the three of us: Morris (Minor) Applethwaite, Bernard (Conkers) Conklin, and I, William Whimsey (they call me Old Bill), decided we wanted to get in on the fun.

Conkers, of course, had to object. It isn't that he's an objectionable sort of fish, is Conkers; he just likes to be different. As a general rule, he's one of the most agreeable fellows I know. Third most agreeable, I'd say. No, I tell a lie: he's the fourth most agreeable. I was forgetting Jonas Crabtree, the tobacconist on the corner. Not your corner, of course, but my corner. Well, of course, it may be your corner, as well; I don't know where you live, after all, do I? No, I tell you quite frankly, I do not.

At any rate, Conkers said, "Look here, why should we do what everybody else is doing?"

"Because, you mutton-headed booby," said Minor, who tended to be brusque when thwarted, "everybody else is doing it. That's rather the point, isn't it?"

You may have noticed that I stayed out of it. I'm an observer of human nature. I was born that way, I suppose. They tell me I didn't even speak for the better part of the first three years of my life, I was so absorbed in observation. I'd still rather watch than participate, especially in work.

At any rate, I was busily observing Minor and Conkers eying one another with a wary willingness to come to blows if no better entertainment offered itself, when Conkers made his brilliant (he does have these flashes of brilliance sometimes, like lightning in a thick cloud) — I forgot where I was. Oh, yes, Conkers made his brilliant suggestion.

"Why don't we do the same thing, only different? Why don't we travel the route by balloon?"

Minor gave a rather unattractive snort of laughter. Minor fancies himself a bitter, saturnine man of the world, master of sarcastic wit.

"A balloon? A balloon, you poor lunatic?"

I thought it was high time I dove in and straightened out the conversation. It often falls to me to do so. It hardly seems fair that one out of three should always be the voice of sweet reason, but there it is. I like to think I bear the burden gracefully.

"Yes, you unmitigated ass," I said, "a balloon! A dirigible! A blimp! An airship, you fool!"

Minor's jaw dropped at the beauty of the thought. "Where would we get one?"

Conkers said, "We would rent one, you know."

"Who would fly it?"

"Old Bill would," said Conkers.

"Old Bill?" the disbelief in Minor's voice would have

hurt me deeply, if I hadn't said the same thing at the same time in the same tone.

"Of course!" Conkers looked at the two of us as if we were idiots. "Old Bill can drive a steamcar without putting it into the ditch above twice in ten miles. If he can do that, it should be child's play for him to drive something that doesn't need a road."

Minor and I were much struck by the simple good sense of Conkers' logic.

I clapped my hands together and rubbed them in anticipatory glee. "Well, then," I said. "All we need now is a dog."

Minor tapped out his pipe tobacco in the fire (he knows I hate that), and said, "Must it be a terrier?"

The three men in a boat had a terrier, you see.

"I could borrow my Aunt Louisa's terrier," I said.

Minor recovered his habitual scorn. "A terrier in an airship? As mad as terriers are for jumping about?"

"My Aunt Louisa's terrier is an irritating dog," I said, thoughtfully. "Not to put too fine a point upon it—"

"Murder your aunt's dog on your own time," said Minor, rather ungenerously, I thought. "If we were to murder every irritating terrier we came across, we'd never do anything else. We won't take a terrier."

"What, then? Do you have a dog in mind?"

That was when Conkers had his second flash of brilliance in one evening. "We could buy a clockwork one. I saw one at the second-hand shop, the last time I pawned my watch."

"Did you, by Jove," said I.

"It isn't in the best shape, but I tried it, and it does work, after a fashion."

Minor had to quibble over trifles: "What sort of a dog is it made to be?"

"The chap claimed it was meant to be a Cavalier King Charles Spaniel."

"Oh," said Minor, pacified. "Cheerful little dogs. Right-o!"

So we were agreed. We would rent a small airship and we would take a clockwork dog.

The provisions were simple. Although the three men in the boat took along a portable cooker and all manner of nonsense, we would take bread, apples, cheese (of the mildest odor obtainable), and a large flask of hot tea. We wouldn't want to sleep in the air, of course, so we would sink with the sun — land in the evening, I mean to say, you know — and take rooms. We would find a good local pub and have some simple fare and as much beer as we could hold. Unlike the poor blighters on the river, we could go inland and avoid the crowd and the price gouging.

Brilliant!

⊛ ⊕ ⊛

The day of our trip dawned, and we found our bespoke conveyance ready and waiting when we pulled up in my steamcar. As soon as Minor and Conkers had released their grips on whatever bits of the 'car they had clutched during the ride, we transferred our clothes boxes and hamper from the boot of the 'car into the airship's wickerwork gondola.

It wasn't overlarge, especially with the coal boxes, and it creaked alarmingly. It smelt distressingly of old straw, dry mold, and mechanical oil. The balloony bit loomed over the open basket.

Minor took exception to the openness, although we had discussed it earlier in relation to the propensity of terriers for jumping. No doubt he hadn't been listening. He seldom listens to anybody else, so it would hardly be implausible to suppose he didn't listen to himself, either. He would have far less profit in it if he did.

"I say," he growled, thrusting his chest out at the weedy little airship rental agent, "what do you mean by foisting this off onto us? Where are the bally windows? Where's the roof, eh? Do you expect us to go up and about in all winds and weathers with no protection? Eh?"

"Oh, 'scuse me, yer lor'ship," the man said with a sneer that could take first prize at any sneering contest anyone cared to sponsor, "I di'n't know money was no object."

Minor lost color at the mention of money changing hands. He harrumphed and turned away. "Very well, then," he said. "Let that be a lesson to you."

The man tipped me a wink and set about explaining the principles of inflating, deflating, fueling, and steering the contraption. Fairly simple, really: lightweight, semi-rigid envelope construction, blah-blah-blah, coal in here both heats the air in the envelope and powers the motors, umpty-umpty, propellers on each side in the rear, so-on-so-forth, rudder, etc.

We crossed his palm with the requisite silver, climbed in, donned the goggles he rented us for a small additional fee, waited for him to cast off (or whatever one calls untying the mooring rope and tossing it into the gondola), I fiddled with the appropriate thingummy, and we were off!

Ah! What could compare with the joy of that ascent? What a thrill, to watch the sad old world fall away beneath us, as if we were birds hitherto mired in the clinging mud of everyday toil and care, suddenly freed and soaring where our souls yearn to go and where our spirits precede us! Who among us has not longed to spread our wings and fly, rising above the grind of present circumstances to the very height of our ability and possibility? Who among us has not dreamed of it, waking or sleeping?

"Good Lord," Conkers shouted into my ear. "Nobody ever told me it would be so flaming LOUD!"

And it was loud, too, between the engines and the wind of our passage humming against the struts and ropes and the hot air exhausting up into the blimpy whatsit.

The tiresome chap who rented us the blimp had tried to insist that we forget about following the Thames and, instead, follow the coast south and west and around to Cornwall, where we could land at his cousin's shipyard, spend our holiday aground, and take the train back to London. I tried to explain to him that the whole point of the expedition was to spend our holiday in the air above the Thames, but he droned on about prevailing winds and half-wits being blown out to sea and brigands with their own airships and such rot as that. It does drive me so wild, when someone gabbles on and on about something of no earthly interest to me, doesn't it you?

I had to admit, though (to myself, of course; I wouldn't have admitted it aloud to those two jackanapes, even if they could have heard me over the noise), that I was having the devil of a time steering or making any headway. The bothersome machine would drift south, until we were moving with extreme slowness along the bank of the river, then parallel to the river, then within sight of the river. The farther south we drifted, the faster (or, rather, the less snail-like) we moved ahead, until we were following the coast, with Cornwall somewhere ahead.

⊛ ⊕ ⊛

We landed at Bognor Regis. The pier looked spiffing,

lights shining on the darkening water like so many acts of kindness in an unkind world. Conkers wanted to hare off and play skittles or some such foolishness, but Minor and I persuaded him — at full volume, to be heard over the engines and so on — that our money (what little the blimp man had left us) would be better spent on food and, more to the point, beer. We had just bumped to a landing that I still maintain was a good one at an all-night airship facility and were still luxuriating in the relative stillness when Minor said,

"I say, whatever became of that deuced dog? Don't tell me we've come off without him?"

"Oh!" said Conkers. "The dog! Yes, he's here, somewhere."

He rummaged around in the luggage, spilling a sack of buns and treading one underfoot, and came up with a rather shopworn pasteboard box with DOG scratched on it in pencil and, underneath this, "CAVALIER KING CHARLES SPANIEL??" Conkers broke the tape holding the box closed, opened the bent and dirty flaps, reached in, and removed an object roughly the size and general shape of a respectable loaf of bread.

He placed it on the floor of the gondola with the air of a cat who has caught something and presented it to you as a gift, though is having second thoughts about it even as he does so.

"If that's all it does," said Minor, "you might as well put it back in the box. I could imagine a better dog than that." Since everyone knows, and frequently states, that Minor has no imagination, I thought this statement a bit strong, and I could see by the look on Conkers' face that Conkers thought so, too.

"Wait a bit," Conkers said. "Let me wind him up and

set him off, you know." He unfolded the beast's — or, I should say, the machine's — paws, tail, and head. My uncle Jasper had just such a dog, only a live one, if "live" is the word I want in connection with a creature so somnolent it didn't move even when we set off firecrackers next to it. Uncle Jasper moved, though, and so did we; he would never have caught us, if the butler, who was in league with him, hadn't locked the front door when we weren't looking.

At any rate, Conkers unfolded our dog, turned a screw in its belly, closed and latched the belly covering, and said, "Rex! Good! Boy!"

The thing quivered. Then, with a squeaking of rusty gears, it wove and wobbled to its feet, and the evening light fell full upon it. A Cavalier King Charles Spaniel, as you may know, has long, gently waved, silky hair and drooping ears, the hair generally being black on the body and white on the paws and legs. I am not, by nature, a skeptical man, and I was willing to stretch a point and concede the possibility that this pseudo-animal, in its prime, had been meant to resemble a Cavalier King Charles Spaniel. Now, though, its fur was tangled, matted, and, where it hadn't fallen out or been clipped off in order to remove something apparently even more repellent than the substances still adherent to it, a slightly greenish black and a more than somewhat grayish white. Its ears had been cut short, leaving flaps like those on the sides of deer-stalker hats to cover its earholes.

It lifted a front paw, turned its head toward Conkers, parted its flabby lips, and said, slowly, with a heavy grinding of its mechanism, "Argh! Argh!"

"Well," said Minor, "it isn't a terrier."

⊛ ⊕ ⊛

We didn't have the heart to leave Rex alone, and we

didn't have the nerve to be seen with him, so we switched him off, put him back in the box, and took him with us.

Naturally, everybody in the pub wanted to know what we had in the box.

Isn't it always the way? If you have something that you just ache for people to ask you about — a spelling medal, say, or a newly published slim volume of one's own verses — nobody ever will. But just put a severed head in a hatbox or something, and people will stop you on the street to beg for a peek.

Minor, of course, got rather testy about it. Here's a typical interchange:

Stranger: Eh, what's in the box, an' all?

Minor: It's a dog.

Stranger: A dog? Devil it is! A dog?

Minor: Yes. No doubt even you have heard of them.

Stranger: Alive, is it? Or dead?

Minor: Look in the box and find out.

Sometimes they would, and sometimes they wouldn't. Of course, even then, they didn't know.

Conkers had another of his rare strokes of intelligence and began betting people a pint that they couldn't guess what it was.

A very successful evening, all in all.

❀ ✹ ❀

We woke late the next morning in our room upstairs in the pub. Minor and I woke first, washed, dressed, shaved, and brought the polished boots in from the hall.

Together, we contemplated the revolting figure of Conkers, sprawled on his cot, drooling into his pillow, unshaven, uncleansed, unclothed (except, of course, for his nightshirt).

Minor turned from the hideous vision and opened the box. Using two handkerchiefs (Conkers' and, I found later, mine), he lifted Rex from the box, wound him up, put him on the cot next to Conkers, and switched him on.

"Rex! Wake him up!"

Rex came to his feet in a series of jerks. He stepped over the jumble of covers, tail-stump quivering. At Conkers' head, he pawed at the inert jaw. "Argh! Argh!" When Conkers didn't respond, Rex delighted us (Minor and me, I mean, not Conkers) by sticking his disintegrating rubber nose into Conkers' ear and releasing short puffs of air, giving the effect of snuffling (without, alas, the vital element of animal moistness).

The effect was all we could have hoped. Conkers bucked as if galvanized. Poor Rex flew off the bed and landed with a clank on the floor, where he spun in slow circles until I righted him with my socked foot.

"Good dog," I said.

Rex opened his jaws and unfurled a flannel tongue which appeared to have been used as a pen-wiper. "Argh! Argh!"

When Conkers finally ceased inventing new curses and had made himself as presentable as one could reasonably expect of him, we went downstairs to a bite of breakfast and — I would say "a hair of the dog that bit us," meaning, you know, a mouthful or two of ale to clear away the cobwebs left by the ale of the night before, but the thought of the hair of the dog we had with us made that figure of speech excessively unappealing — a mouthful or two of ale.

The pubkeeper had a word of advice for us, of course. Haven't you noticed that, whenever one is doing something, other people who are not doing it always have great heaping slathers of advice on how one should do it?

"Better stay close to the coast around here," he said. "It's safe enough just above land, but The Pirates of Bognor Regis skirt the beach, waiting for some nodcock to be blown just far enough out to sea for 'em to catch."

I thanked him, of course: one doesn't want to antagonize the chap preparing one's food and drink, after all, but shared a knowing wink with my fellow aeronauts.

⊛ ⊛ ⊛

Goggles in place, faithful dog whirring and clanking at the far end of the gondola, we fired up the engines and lifted off.

The elegant public buildings of Bognor Regis fell away below us.

"I say," Conkers shouted over the sound of the engines, "can you lower this a bit and go closer to the beach?"

"Why would I do that?" Everyone wants to tell one how to steer. It's enough to drive one mad.

"Girls," said Conkers. "Sea bathing."

Really, Conkers can be quite sensible, when he puts his mind to it.

I reduced the heat being channeled to the envelope (that's what we blimp-men call the balloon thing, you know) and pointed our nose to sea.

"Stop here! Stop here!" Minor and Conkers both screeched, as if volume would make a difference.

"It's all very well for you to say, 'Stop here,' but I can only control the rudder," I said, "not the ruddy wind!"

For, as I turned broadside to the beach, the wind caught the envelope and we slid sideways out and away from land.

"You muffleheaded chump!" Minor strode toward me. "Here — give me the rudder! Upon my word, my grandmother could steer better than you!"

"Bring your grandmother aboard, and I'll give her the rudder, but I jolly well won't give it to such a gormless duffer as you!"

As we struggled over control of the steering mechanism, I gradually became aware of Conkers' silly voice droning, "Chaps! I say, chaps! Here, you two! I say!"

When we paused to recruit our strength for another bout, Minor rounded on him.

"What is it, you bleating nitwit?"

Conkers only stared, seeming to be riveted by some sight behind us.

Minor and I turned.

A huge black airship with a white skull and crossbones emblazoned on the side was closing on us. It was near enough for us to see the evil grins of the men and women of the crew and the glint of their goggles.

Minor and I each let go of the rudder. In concert, we each said, "You take it! I'll add coal!"

We each lunged for the coal scuttle, bounced off each other, and fell to the gondola's floor. Dispossessed straw rose around us in a musty cloud.

"This is no time for you chaps to practice music hall routines," Conkers said. "I believe we're about to be boarded."

A grappling hook flew over the side of our basket and fastened firmly in the wickerwork. There was a violent jounce as it afixed itself and began pulling us toward the sinister vessel. A tell-tale clack and whizz spoke of Rex having tipped over and of his hapless struggle to right himself without the aid of a friendly toe.

Before one could say "Jack Robinson," which would

have been a fairly useless thing to have said at such a time, the pirate ship was snugged against ours and a massive, muscular chap had joined us. He was flanked by two lieutenants, one male and one female, each brandishing muscles and flexing pistols. Er, the other way 'round, I think I mean.

Conkers stammered, "W-why? We aren't a cargo ship, you know. We aren't wealthy, or from wealthy families. Why capture us?"

The pirate chief's evil grin grew wider and, if possible, more evil.

"I can always use another ship for my fleet, even assuming you have no money with you, and you off on holiday. Then there's your food supplies. It may not be much, but it's something, eh? And don't underestimate the pleasure of watching you beg for your lives, and the diversion of wagering on how many times each of you will resurface before you drown."

Conkers spoke for us all: "Oh, I say!"

There was really nothing to add to that.

Apparently, Rex had managed to recover his feet, for he chose that moment to approach, stiff-legged, perhaps in response to some vestige of programming that instructed him to protect the person and property of his owner.

"Argh! Argh!" A low-pitched grating sound, possibly meant to be a growl, followed.

The pirate chief's grey eyes bulged and his jaw dropped. Had he never seen a clockwork dog before, or did he (and this was my preferred hypothesis) not realize that a clockwork dog is what he saw?

Both suppositions proved false, for he said,

"Rex! Rex, old boy!" The pirate chief sank to one knee,

arms outstretched.

Rex hobbled over to him and allowed him to scoop him up, close to what one would previously have laid good odds was a heartless chest. Rex' flannel tongue swiped dry licks across the pirate's tear-dampened cheeks, leaving faint streaks of blue-black ink upon them.

The chief turned to his lieutenants. "This is Rex! My dear old playfellow! Often, I've told you how it crushed me when my uncle, whose ward I was, gave him away when I was in school."

The lieutenants looked as if they remembered very well, and that it had been jolly near once too often.

"Yes," one of them said. "Oxford, I believe. Senior year."

"It's why I became a pirate," said the vicious brute cuddling the clockwork canine. "I was trying — vainly, pitifully — to fill the void left by his loss. And here he is!"

It was all very touching, but I hope I won't be accused of lacking sentiment when I say that I was still somewhat concerned about our immediate future — mine and Minor's and Conkers', I mean.

"Go back aboard the ship," said the chief to his underlings. "Divide my share of all our loot amongst you. I mean to return to land with these lubbers, and lead a blameless life evermore."

He got no argument. In two shakes of a lamb's tail (though I don't see that a lamb shakes its tail at a greater velocity than any other frolicsome mammal), the pirates had left us, we were free of the grappling hook, and Rex' old master was plying the winds and easing us back to shore.

Once we landed, he put us out, took all our money, food, and clothes (except for what we wore — one is, cutthroat or not, a gentleman), and informed us that he was taking the blimp to sell on the black market.

I pointed out a logical fallacy in that course of behavior: "I thought you meant to lead a blameless life evermore."

"True," he said, "but one must have a start."

A forceful argument, its persuasiveness bolstered by the pistol which he had retained from his life as a pirate.

"Will you leave us nothing?" Conkers can put on a convincing show of injured innocence. I've seen him stand before a mirror, practicing it, for hours before going to face a creditor. It usually buys him a few days' grace, and it didn't fail him, now.

A familiar pasteboard box sailed over the gondola's side, clattering as it landed in my arms.

"Not your old playfellow, surely!"

"Seeing him again brought me the closure I needed," said the former pirate. "Now, I must travel light. Farewell!"

From within the box, Rex answered, "Argh!"

⊛ ⊛ ⊛

We reported the theft, of course, and the police took to the skies in pursuit of the renegade. We never heard the result, but our flight insurance indemnified us against piracy, so at least we didn't have to reimburse the balloon chappie for the airship.

We finished our holiday in my own cozy rooms, pipes in our mouths, feet on the hob, dog snoring with a gentle birr.

"After all," said Minor, speaking for all of us, "there's no place like home."

"Very true," I said, eying the last of my bottled beer as it slid down Minor's gullet. "Why don't you go there?"

The End

TRACER'S CHOICE

DANI J. CAILE

From his table in the Atlantic Royal Corps' first class restaurant he not only had a bird's eye view of the ocean some hundred meters below, with the shape of the Zeppelin shimmering on the surface, but also of the gartered leg of the young woman sitting across from him, a glimpse of a golden Derringer showing through the cut of her draped skirt. Southern gal, recently widowed, if the drab colours gave a clue. Perhaps she was yet another young bride from the war, marrying her schoolyard sweetheart before he went off to fight and fall in battle. She still wore the ring, but why the piece?

A waiter broke the spell.

"Would sir care for another tea?"

Tracer pushed his empty cup towards the uniformed chap with the heel of his dirty boot, indicating a refill. After pouring, and with a little cough, the waiter left. Tracer lifted his eyes to the other passengers, who turned and continued with their business, leaving him to get back to polishing Amelie's leather sight cover with his own homemade dubbin. As he occasionally drank his Earl Grey, the sound of the oiled revolutions from the Zeppelin's motor gears and the occasional burst of steam emanating from the exhaust ports soothed and comforted him. Bounder's voice, however, did not.

"Why can't you use some of that on your boots, Tracer? They're filthy. Look at them!"

Tracer stopped his buffing and looked Bounder dead in the eyes. "In the trenches, we learnt quickly that an ounce of dubbin on your weapon is worth a million polished rivets on your blazer."

Tracer laughed at his own joke as his partner shifted uneasily in one of the restaurant's exquisitely embroidered oak chairs. Clean, immaculate, inexperienced. Three words that summed up Bounder. Ponce. Four.

"Uncle said you were rude and obnoxious. I tend to agree."

Tracer went back to his polishing.

"Besides, we have no need for weapons on this journey. It is merely a delivery of a letter."

"Uncle" was Tracer's boss, Dunst, a small-time gangster with big-time connections in Washington State. Tracer didn't want to take this job, but maybe it would pay enough to fix his busted leg, now encased in the latest copper-piping cast money could buy, allowing him some mobility for the first time after being shot three times in the femur by the Norman brothers some weeks back. Their funeral was a blast, with Wagner's 'Lohengrin' drifting through the pews. They were well respected, but crooks all the same.

"I never go anywhere without my dear Amelie by my side."

"Amelie? You were specifically told not to bring any-one el—"

Tracer lifted the double barrel of his beloved and trusted

rifle into plain view.

"Please! Not at the table! Tracer, your manners are abominable. Why my Uncle asked you to come along is beyond me!"

"To babysit, I reckon."

Bounder pushed his chair back and stood up from their table. Tracer saw he wanted to retort but had thought better of it. Instead, he took out his platinum Bennett pocket watch, its engraved casing encrusted? with diamonds, and checked the time.

"We're arriving in fifteen minutes at Hamilton. From there, we take a boat. I expect to see you at the departation ramp in ten."

Tracer gave a nod. He was happy to see his partner leave, allowing him to finish his polishing and continue to watch. . . . The young woman was already up, walking back to the first class deck. A shame. She moved graciously and with style. As she passed through the restaurant's double doors, Tracer was sure she took a moment to look back.

Twenty-five minutes later, and about halfway down the ramp, Tracer's copper cast stuck between the wooden ruts. With one forceful wrench, he ripped it out, sending wood into the water. Bounder tutted as he drew nearer.

"Sometimes metal and wood don't mix."

"Especially when you're around, Tracer. Wait here and try not to break anything. I'll go and look for our ride."

As Bounder left, the young woman from the restaurant, sunshade in hand, made it down the ramp, sidestepping the hole. She nodded to him in recognition. Tracer touched his worn bowler hat.

"Ma'am."

To his disappointment, the woman was met by a smartly

dressed man and led away to one of the many steam-powered carts parked around the harbour. Tracer was surprised at the reach of the Industrial Revolution. Hamilton, a town so far from the mainland, was still hit hard, with many carts of all shapes and sizes puffing along the main street, filling the air with soot and smoke. Only the occasional palm tree reminded him that they weren't in Baltimore anymore.

"Found it, come on."

Bounder pointed further down the harbour and they walked on, watching the Zeppelin depart, continuing to its next destination somewhere in the West Indies. It left a trail of neat steam clouds which hung motionless in the air for a moment before being dissipated by the turning rotors. Tracer heard the whirring of gears and the burn of the furnace as it gained height, the sound disappearing as the ship became a mere speck in the sky. Damn British. At least the Americans had the Pacific. One day he'd travel American; their ships had more of a "je ne sais quoi" about them, and they flew the flag.

A group of dirty street urchins broke the moment and mobbed them, screaming and hollering, turning them around and leaving in a cloud of dust. Tracer checked his belongings, a victim of many such attacks in the cities, but of course he had nothing to steal. Bounder, on the other hand, had much to learn.

"They took my pocket watch! Hey!"

"Forget about it; you can buy another one. Out here in the sticks, I guess they don't get much."

"Don't get much? Look around you, don't you notice the abundance of wealth and business in the harbour, the ships of all shapes, sizes and places of origin?"

Bounder was right; they were walking through a bustling port filled to full capacity.

"Oh yeah. Why's that?"

"Ah, you know nothing of the world of trade, do you, Tracer?"

Five words. Smartarse.

"There aren't any custom taxes here, not like on the mainland. A man, if he's lucky and clever, can make a million standing right on this very spot."

They stood there for a while as merchandise was being loaded onto and unloaded from the ships around them, with Bounder looking out for the urchins, hoping to get back his watch. He finally gestured Tracer over to a smaller boat a few hundred meters away.

"Here it is. Ahoy!" Bounder greeted a sailor who was sitting inside the small copper and wood steam powerboat. In addition to its fine smooth lines, it was decorated from bow to stern with brass decals and motifs emulating mythical creatures of the deep: mermaids, giant octopi and other such sea monsters. The sailor bowed and gave a helping hand to them both as they boarded the small craft. On its side, Tracer saw a small decorative plate with the name "Hestia II".

Without a word, the sailor stoked the small boiler and built up steam. As he fixed the rotor shaft to reverse, the boat left the dock slow and steady, turning around to head out to sea. With a shift of a lever, the boat continued forwards out of the harbour. An hour later, they had reached their destination, the large steam-powered personal yacht of the recipient of the letter, moored north of Bermuda. The name on the side read the same as the smaller boat, except for number, "Hestia I". It was a magnificent boat in a class of its own: three tiers, two masts, with one large funnel at the stern. The windows were mostly stained glass with intricate designs which caused ripple pattern effects on the surface of the water.

"Now, this one's nice, but that's a beaut."

Tracer always appreciated beauty, no matter what shape or form it came in.

"The 'Hestia I'. I've heard a lot about it, but seeing is believing."

Two more sailors appeared on deck and helped them climb aboard.

"How many employed men does this man have?"

"Professor Schutzheimer is a wealthy man, Tracer. He can have as many as he wishes. Though I have heard that he's a ladies' man."

As the words came from Bounder's mouth, a threesome of the most luscious feminine creatures Tracer had ever seen walked by them on deck.

"You see? He has taste."

"Hell, yeah!"

Their eyes elsewhere, they missed the smart but aged butler standing before them.

"Greetings, gentlemen. Professor Schutzheimer is at present occupied. If you would please wait inside, he will be with you shortly." The butler gestured them into a lavish room, presumably an office of sorts, and they sat on opposite ends of a large brown leather sofa facing the Professor's desk. A world map hung behind the desk, with the best cartography Tracer had ever seen. The room itself was laid from wall to wall with a huge Serapi carpet and the dark oak furniture was covered with little odds and ends: statues, portraits and many copper and brass valves, pipes, pistons and other bits of machinery that Tracer couldn't recognise. He wasn't an engineer; he was a gunman.

Two bookcases filled with some of the greatest writers of the time — Brontë, Dostoyevsky, Shelley, Hugo, to name but a few — moved, and a man Tracer supposed to be the Professor came through the opening. With one glance around the room, the Professor sat down in his luxurious leather chair behind his even more opulent desk.

"Ah, guests from the mainland! Please, take a seat . . . oh, I see you have . . . now, let me take a closer look. . . ."

The old man scrutinised the two seated men. Tracer rested Amelie on a large mahogany inlaid writing desk.

"A blue tunic with frog fastenings and braid trim? I wouldn't have guessed you were a Hussar. Especially with those boots."

Sitting more upright, Tracer tried to remember where he picked up this jacket of his, perhaps from Tricky Géza in downtown Baltimore.

"And the other, a French dandelion, if I'm not mistaken, by the latest Parisian fashion."

Bounder seemed happy that the Professor had caught onto his passion for Parisian fashion.

"Paris! Why, yes, I. . . . dandelion?"

The Professor ignored Bounder's reply, turning rather to Tracer until there was silence.

"So, what's new in the big US of A, my dear fellows?"

Tracer beat Bounder to the punch.

"Doing fine, just fine. Taxes are up, unemployment is up, crime is. . . ."

Bounder gestured Tracer to be quiet. He obliged, for now.

"Excellent, Professor, excellent. Things are looking up;

the 38 stars and stripes fly with pride."

"Good, good. It's very nice of you to visit, but, if I may enquire, why are you here?"

This was Bounder's territory. Tracer looked through the windows, hoping to catch another glimpse of those nubiles.

"As much as I'd like to say it is an honour to be here in your presence. . . ."

"You may."

". . . we have come to deliver a letter from my Uncle, Mr. Dunst of Washington."

The name drop didn't make the impact Bounder had probably hoped for.

"Dunst? Oh yes, I have heard of that name in darker corners of society. If I may?"

Bounder reached into his spotless sack coat and took out the sealed letter, passing it to the Professor. With an ornate knife from his desk, the man broke the seal and read.

"Interesting."

"Really?"

Tracer lifted his dirty boots up on the corner of the writing desk, only for Schutzheimer to give him a finger shake of disapproval.

"Please."

Tracer put his feet back down and sat upright again.

"Yes, it is interesting how fast information travels in such a short time. I have not yet refined the machine and already the offers are fluttering in. You are the second today."

"Offers?" asked Bounder.

"Second?" queried Tracer. How did someone beat them to this boat today? As far as he knew, Hamilton only received one Zeppelin per day.

"Yes. You do not know the contents of this letter?"

"No, we are merely messengers."

"Quite. But! A chance!"

The Professor looked very happy, jumping up from his comfortable chair and taking out a copy of Tolstoy's War and Peace from the left bookshelf. It had to be that masterpiece; no other book was that thick. Yet another secret door opened and the Professor disappeared down a flight of stairs.

"Come this way, if you please."

Tracer wasn't happy to follow a strange old man through a secret door, but where could it lead? At best, to the bottom of the boat. He couldn't have been more wrong.

Bounder was the first to state the obvious.

"This is going down a bit far, isn't it?"

Tracer was happy he'd flung Amelie onto his back before they'd left.

"Quite. How very observant of you."

The Professor hummed a few bars of something Tracer had never heard, the sound echoing through the tubular staircase.

"Rather good, I think. A friend of mine wrote this, still hasn't finished it yet, though. He's thinking of calling it 'the American'."

It had a certain charm. Tracer took care not to bang Amelie on the side of the ever-shrinking tube. They finally arrived at a circular door which the Professor opened by turning the locking wheel and releasing a lever. Tracer looked up and saw the pinprick of light above. By his reckoning, they might have travelled down to the ocean floor. Steam and heat hit them as the Professor entered whatever it was below. Bounder went after him; Tracer reluctantly followed.

"And here she is! Isn't she beautiful?"

Professor Schutzheimer hugged what looked like a large metallic boiler, shiny and covered in a mass of copper and brass fittings. Tracer and Bounder both tried to show some interest. The Professor tapped some dials and tweaked a valve or two.

"Fantastic, Prof . . . err . . . what is it?" asked Tracer.

Bounder got closer to the machine and was awarded with a faceful of hot steam.

"The reason you are here, the reason we are all here, eh, dear fellows?"

Tracer found a small tripod to sit on; his bad leg was giving him grief from all those stairs.

"What exactly does it do, Prof?"

"Ah! The million dollar question."

The Professor examined Tracer's copper cast and laughed.

"Remind me later, I'll fix that up for you."

"Thanks. Now, what is this?"

"Infinite energy."

"What?"

"Infinite energy, or as near as damnit for what I can do, running at. . . ."

The Professor checked a few more dials.

". . . running at 97.4 % efficiency. Not bad, not bad at all."

"What do you mean, Professor, 'infinite energy'?" Bounder tried to enter the conversation.

"Just what I say. This little beau—"

From where Tracer was sitting, it wasn't so little. The room they were in wasn't so wide but it stretched as far as the eye could see.

". . . uses less than 5% of the energy that the best steam

engines on today's market do, through the use of an extensive system of ever-diminishing pistons, valves and steam cooling and heating the pipes. It's taken me twelve years to get this far, and I'm almost ready to make my machine public."

Bounder stood speechless, so Tracer tried to see if he understood the Professor.

"So this 'little' beauty runs on much less fuel than an ordinary engine?"

"Yes. Got it in one. Excellent, dear boy, I see you are the brains of the team. In addition, seawater is allowed to enter through purifiers heated by the main boiler, whereas there is also a constant source of heat from the underwater geysers situated just below us, which is regulated here using a series of valves and dials which I supervise on a daily basis. This wonderful machine can run almost continuously."

"That's amazing! But, Prof, there's just one thing. It's huge."

All three looked down towards the end of the machine.

"As I already said, it has taken me twelve years to get this far. A little more time and I'm sure I could shrink it a little. Once this problem is solved, I will convert it over to land-based fuels and 'Hey Presto'! It will revolutionise the industries and the world as we know it!"

They were silent for a moment.

"Can you feel the magnitude of it all?"

"Not really. Shrink it a little, you say?" asked Bounder.

The Professor took Bounder by the shoulder and indicated for Tracer to follow.

"This fine engine is what your letter is about. Your uncle wishes to buy the patent, once it is available."

Bounder finally woke up.

"Oh, I see . . . why?"

The Professor looked back at Tracer.

"Was he dropped on his head as a baby?"

"Wouldn't know."

"My dear fellow. . . ."

Tracer looked up the flight of stairs and sighed. That was going to hurt. The Professor pulled a lever by the side of the door and a platform appeared, big enough for all three of them to stand on, at a squeeze.

"Your uncle intends to have control of this patent. I, however, would like to make sure it is sold to the correct buyer, one who would 'bring it to light' to benefit society, so to speak, and not 'hide it away'. Which do you think your uncle is?"

The Professor closed the circular door, spinning the wheel to lock, and turned the lever, sending the platform along the gradient of the stairs and lifting them up the tube. Tracer's sigh was now one of relief, with no need to climb. They were back in the office in minutes. The platform automatically went back down.

"Only upwards, I'm afraid. One must get one's exercise somewhere, mustn't one?"

The Professor sat back down in his chair, staring at the two men.

"Telegraph your uncle as to his intention and we shall await his reply. Until then, you may stay on my yacht, if you so wish."

"You've got wireless telegraph on your yacht, Prof?" As far as Tracer knew, it still had its teething problems.

"Why, of course. Isn't it amazing what you can do today? We were using only pigeons a few years ago and now electromagnetic waves? Amazing, absolutely amazing."

A sailor came in and the Professor whispered something. The sailor addressed Bounder.

"Sir, please step this way. Professor Schutzheimer's telegraph room is at your disposal."

"Thank you. And thank you, Professor, we will of course take you up on your kind offer."

Tracer leant over to Bounder. "Eh?"

"We're staying."

The Professor got up to leave.

"Excellent. I will assign you your own cabins and please be punctual for dinner tonight. 8 o'clock sharp."

They nodded to the Professor as he left.

"Come on, Tracer, I've got a telegraph to send."

"You want me to hold your hand for you?"

"Oh, shut up and just follow."

Tracer couldn't remember the last time he'd slept on a boat. Or held someone's hand.

The dinner was something Tracer had rarely experienced before. Two main courses with a huge range of dishes from pork, lamb, beef and fish, the latter being the main part, and Venetian glass bowls of sorbet and ice cream between each dish, all served by half a dozen of the Professor's sailors, doubling as footmen for the evening. Tracer was frightened to use the cutlery on the china, it was that delicate and 'sophisticated'. He was also a little shaky from not having Amelie with him. Light quartet music played throughout, giving the place a dignified atmosphere. However, he and Bounder weren't the only ones dining. There was the Mayor of Hamilton with his dear wife and daughter, a sickly looking thing; the Commander in Chief of the local British garrison with his other half; and a number of the most influential and wealthy individuals from the island. It was quite a crowd of stuck-up snobs; Bounder probably felt right at home. Professor Schutzheimer leant over to Tracer.

"Like the spread? It's called 'a la russe' in French, you know."

"I call it a lot of food. How can you eat it all? There's so much of it."

"Ah, never you mind, my dear fellow. We always send what is left to the poor on the island. There are some among the people. Somewhere."

"Oh, how the other half lives."

"Half?"

With their bellies full and plates empty, the chef was allowed to enter and be congratulated on his achievement.

"Ladies and gentlemen, let me please introduce you to the hero of the night, Auguste from Paris."

They all applauded the chef for the excellent and sumptuously rich meal.

"I 'poached' him from the Savoy."

A few of the more eager merchants laughed at the Professor's remark.

"And now . . . a small performance. Please, this way, ladies and gentlemen."

Tracer followed the crowd out of the dining area, up some red carpeted stairs and into a small ballroom with three crystal chandeliers hanging from the mirrored ceiling. The quartet had re-assembled on a stage in front of a collection of chairs, every one of them a work of art. Tracer sat at the back; he was a little wary of the Commander in Chief. He was sure the man's face was familiar, a face from somewhere in his sordid history. Tracer couldn't quite place him. The war? Some other action elsewhere?

The music started, a peculiar mix from what Tracer

recognised, one piece from Goetz and another from Verdi, but the rest? Nonetheless, the performance was relaxing; even with his suspicions of the company, Tracer began to drop the hard shell he always held around himself, the unkept veteran headhunter who'd seen too much, killed too many. Flashes of lost friends and the heat of battle came into his mind, the hard times in the war, that dreaded war. American against American, brother against brother. If it wasn't for Salyersville, it could've ended ten years earlier, saving thousands of lives. Back then, there was a choice: shoot or be shot. Now, life was softer, much softer, yet unclear, no longer the black and white it was. The bridge. There was always the bridge. Fleeing women and children amongst the crossfire, stuck between both sides. His officer tried to destroy the bridge but the fuse wouldn't light. Being the brigade's sharpshooter, Tracer was ordered to blow the charge. There had been no choice.

His nightmarish recollection came to a halt when he heard an off-note from the cellist, not much of one, but enough for the ear of a connoisseur such as himself. Tracer got a shock. It was the woman from the Zeppelin! My, how she got around, now dressed in a lovely white satin evening gown. They swapped glances, though hers was not so forward.

After the small performance, the guests thanked their host one by one and departed on the "Hestia II". The quartet, however, had their own boat and stayed on board for a little while longer. Tracer grabbed his chance when the woman came out for a smoke on the deck.

"Do you mind if I. . . ?" asked Tracer.

"Not at all."

He stood next to her at the rail and took out his tobacco pouch. She was smoking some Vanity Fair while he was always content with his own hand-rolled. She watched him with a sideways glance but mostly gave him the cold shoulder. Completing the roll-up, he took out his leather-bound case of matches and lit the finished article.

"I heard you in there tonight."

The woman gave a cough and smiled shyly his way.

"Oh, the performance?"

"The note."

She flicked some ash over the side.

"I was never one for practise."

"Practise makes perfect."

"Not all of us are, er—"

"Tracer."

He bowed his head a little and she acknowledged him.

"Not all of us are perfectionists, Tracer."

"Quite so."

"Well, other than the one note, did the performance reach your high standards?"

"Uh-huh. Some I'd heard before, some not."

"A man with taste, I see."

They gazed out into the night, the moon reflecting off the surface of the still water.

"A strange name, Tracer."

"Nickname. Got it in the war."

"The war? Are you a fighting man, Tracer?"

"It depends on the price."

She shifted uneasily; it was now or never.

"Might I enquire as to your moniker, madam?"

"You may."

At that, she casually threw the remainder of her cigarette into the water and turned to go.

"Good night, Tracer."

And that was it. No spark, no nothing. No look in the eye, cheap flirt or touching gesture. He was rarely let down so badly, but this? His suave coarseness and dark, mysterious appearance was usually enough to raise at least an eyebrow or two. Upset by her dismissal, he hung on the rail, smoking his roll-up and spitting into the water below. The whole evening churned his stomach; it disgusted him — the decadence, the gluttony of the upper class — it made him sick. How he wished for a night on the town in the dingy streets of Baltimore, with the promise of a warm bed from some floozy he'd pick up in a bar, and the chance of a fight from her jealous ex-lover. Throwing the roach away, he wearily went to his assigned cabin. Tomorrow was the chance of an answer from Dunst.

The night was long. Every few minutes, his leg cramped up in its copper cast and he changed position for some relief. He must've caught only a few minutes of rest in the three hours he'd tried to sleep when he sensed that he wasn't alone. The door was closed. His window was open to let in the fresh sea air, though nothing more. Not even a dwarf could squeeze through the porthole. So what was it? He heard a scraping on the parquet flooring of his cabin and slowly moved over to sneak a look. Something large and shiny flew towards his face and missed him by a hair's width. Retrieving his Bowie knife from under his pillow, he spun around and pinned the creature to the wall above the bed. Its legs jerked and quivered until a puff of steam escaped from its torso. A steam-powered twelve-inch insect? Gears turned their last revolutions as the little machine came to a dead stop. What was this? Whose was this? Was it one of the Professor's toys sent to kill him? And why?

There was no time to think. The whole yacht suddenly

creaked loudly and he fell out of bed. Screams and shouts sounded outside and a bell tolled, Tracer guessing the alarm to abandon ship. Another scream, this one familiar, came from next door. Bounder. Wasting no time, he grabbed Amelie and his shoulder bag, flung on his boots, and crashed through the door separating their cabins.

"Bounder?"

He found his companion on the floor with another of the gruesome little mechanical insects steaming away with a Swiss Army knife in its brass hind shell. Bounder hadn't been so lucky. He was losing some blood from his neck but he was still alive and kicking. Maybe he wasn't as useless as he looked.

"What the hell was that?"

Tracer helped him up and Bounder wrapped a scarf around his own neck, the blood dripping down onto his silk nightwear. They both heard the bell again.

"Boat's going down, Tracer, we have to get outta here!"

Tracer grabbed Amelie and checked the breech. Loaded. He held her smooth wooden stock firmly under his arm. He didn't take kindly to attempts on his life.

"Not before I get some answers."

He ran out of the cabin and onto the deck, pushing past the sailors setting lifeboats onto the water.

"Sir! This way!"

"Not likely!"

Tracer ran further down the port side of the boat. There was a gunshot up ahead, on the next deck. As the boat began to tip, Tracer climbed the nearest ladder and entered what he assumed to be the place from whence it came, the Professor's office. He was correct, and yet again surprised. The Professor had been shot, bleeding on one of his many expensive Persian rugs dotted around the floor, with someone leaning over his dying body. It was the woman, still dressed in her white satin gown and holding in her hand a smoking Derringer.

"You!"

She never looked back, smashing through a window on the starboard side. Tracer lifted Amelie but he was too slow.

"Help me. . . ."

He ran over to the Professor but her aim had been true.

"Sorry, Prof, looks like it's all over. Any last requests?"

Professor Schutzheimer lifted a shaking finger and pointed over to a panel hidden under his desk.

"Close the room, the room below."

Tracer went over to the desk and examined the panel. He flipped the lever, instantly hearing release valves hissing behind the bookshelves. He imagined his action had disconnected the tubular staircase from the yacht. Levers, levers everywhere. . . .

"Good, good. Know any good epitaphs, my dear fellow?"

"No, sorry, but it's a better place you go to, if that's any comfort."

The Professor only smiled and closed his eyes, but Tracer had to know.

"Who was that, Prof? The woman."

"Mmm? Can't I die in peace?"

"No."

Tracer had an idea that it was the woman who'd sent them the deadly mechanical insects; perhaps she had also sabotaged the yacht, as well as killed their host. He knelt down and poked his finger into the bullet hole in the Professor's chest.

"Ahh! Damn you, sir!"

"The woman, Prof?"

Schutzheimer spat blood in his face and Tracer repeated the action.

"Ahh! Okay! She's the daughter of a man I once knew!"

"I see, the plot thickens."

Bounder ran in.

"What's going on? Tracer! The boat is sinking!"

"And? Prof, tell me!"

"Does it really matter? I'm dying! And you'll die, if you don't get out of here fast!"

Tracer poked two fingers into the bullet hole.

"Ahh! All right, all right! His name was Maddison, my research partner back in the 60s! Specialised in steam minatures, toys, I called them. I . . . I left him out of a few patents and I err. . . ."

"You screwed him?"

Silence. Again with the fingers.

"Ahh! Stop that! Yes! He got in the way! He found out about a few dodgy deals I'd made with some Russian entrepreneurs and was going to tell the authorities! What was I meant to do? I was young, ambitious—"

The boat rocked violently, sending all three starboard. Once Tracer had regained his bearings, he looked over at the Professor. Bounder grabbed him by the shoulder.

"He's gone, Tracer! And we should go, too!"

He had a point. Tracer looked out of the broken starboard window where luckily the "Hestia II" was steaming by, manned by one of Schutzheimer's sailors, probably the last to leave.

"Ahoy, there!"

As soon as he heard Tracer's call, the sailor

maneuvered the little steam-powerboat back towards them and took no time to latch on with a rope. Holding onto Amelie, Tracer climbed out of the window frame and jumped from the sloped side of the yacht, hitting the deck of "Hestia II" with both feet. It would have worked just fine without the heavy metal cast on his leg, but the thrice-damned contraption buckled and disintegrated into lethal shards of copper. Amelie was okay, but Tracer lay sprawled on the deck, wincing in pain. Bounder jumped and landed on him.

"Bounder! Get off!"

The sailor at the wheel took the "Hestia II" away from her sinking big sister and headed for the shore.

"What the hell just happened, Tracer?"

"You just crushed my arse!"

"No, in there! What just happened in there?"

"The Prof was shot."

"Who would do such a thing?"

Tracer caught a flash of another boat's helm ahead. There were a few lifeboats dotted around filled with survivors, but this was a powered boat.

"Hey, sailor, shine a light over there, will ya?"

The sailor gave the wheel to Bounder and climbed onto the front of the boat. He lit the front lantern and pointed it ahead.

"Isn't that a woman?" asked Bounder.

"Yes."

Yet again, the same woman, like a bad penny.

"She's the one who just killed the Professor. 'Revenge is a dish best served cold'. Choderlos de LaClos, if I'm not mistaken."

"She killed Schutzheimer?"

French literature was lost on Bounder. Six words. Philistine.

"Yeah. And probably sank the boat, too."

"And the machine?"

"Lost, I guess."

As far as Tracer could tell, the Professor's "beauty" was locked away, deep on the ocean floor.

"Damn it! Uncle trusted me to get it right this time! He's going to have my head for this! Who the hell does she think she is!"

"The daughter of a cheated and murdered man?"

The shore and harbour were still far off but now coming into view. She was pulling away from them, creating distance.

"She's ruined everything!"

Bounder was stomping around on the deck, moving the wheel and causing the boat to shake.

"Steady! Calm down, Bounder!"

"Shoot her, damn it! Shoot her!"

"What?"

"That's an order, Tracer! Shoot the damn bitch!"

Tracer eyed up the distance, measured the bobbing of each boat and lifted Amelie, resting her on the front wooden deck and setting his eye to her sights. The shot was possible. He watched as her white satin gown flurried in the light sea breeze.

"Shoot her!"

Choices, choices.

CONTRIBUTORS

Marian Allen For as long as she can remember, Marian Allen has loved telling and being told stories. When, at the age of about six, she was informed that somebody got paid for writing all those books and movies and television shows, she abandoned her previous ambition (beachcomber), and became a writer.

Dani J. Caile is a teacher and proofreader (BA in Philology specialising in Pedagogy) who is currently residing in Budapest, Hungary. After a lifetime of reading clones and a decade of proofreading coffee table books, in retaliation he has written 4 fantasy books and 1 novella, including "Man by a tree", "The Bethlehem Fiasco", "The Rage of Atlantis", "TDX2", and "Manna-X", all based on his own Neo-Plantonic universe. His latest work, "How to build a castle in seven easy steps", is under submission now. He has also published 2 short story compilations, based on The Iron Writer Challenge, on Smashwords.com called "Dani's Shorts" and "Dani's Shorts 2", available for free. When not writing, directing and dabbling in Shakespeare, teaching English, proofreading, washing up, hoovering, and driving all over the place, he is busy with his loving and long-suffering family.

K.A. DaVur was born and raised in an extremely haunted house near the wild and wooded banks of Lake Michigan. She won her first writing competition at the age of six and has never looked back, filling a seemingly endless series of notebooks and journals with fantastical stories and even a poem or two. She next attended Transylvania University in Lexington, Kentucky, the only university in the United States to boast no less than two former faculty members entombed under the steps of the administration building. Ms. DaVur has traveled extensively throughout the Midwest leading writing workshops based on that book at youth camps, elementary schools, and children's museums. She currently resides in the woods of Indiana where she enjoys writing novels, working on her hobby farm and homeschooling her four miniature vampire stalkers.

Katina French is a science fiction and fantasy author from southern Indiana. An award-winning copywriter, she's been writing professionally for over 20 years. Recent works include "The Clockwork Republics Series," a set of steampunk retellings of classic fairy tales, as well as the space adventure serial BELLE STARR.

Her novella, Bitter Cold, was featured in the Echelon Press anthology ONCE UPON A CLOCKWORK TALE, which debuted in the Amazon Top 100 for Steampunk.

Ms. French writes fast-paced, humor-laced adventure stories with a touch of mystery and romance that appeal to young adults and the young at heart.

She lives near Louisville, Kentucky with her husband, and two children.

Thomas Lamkin Jr. was born in a small town in Arizona, and moved from place to place until settling back down in Louisville, Kentucky, near where previous generations of his family had lived. This blend of the new and the familiar gives him the ability to see the region through fresh eyes that still understand the history and the culture of the people. This sense of wonder and connection comes through in his photography, art, and stories. Early in his life, Thomas had the love of adventure and ability to see beyond the obvious instilled in him by his father. Thomas grew up on epic stories, some of them originals, just now being put to paper, and because of this, pursued a degree in Creative Writing from University of North Carolina. His goal remains to tell stories, whatever medium may present itself. You may view his work at www.tljonline.com.

Sara Marian was raised in the woods by wild English teachers, and has been writing for as long as she can remember. She is an avid reader of a wide range of fiction, especially classic literature, fantasy, and historical fiction mysteries. She is pursuing a degree in anthropology from University of Louisville (minoring in Russian studies), with plans for a career in archaeology.

Brick Marlin has been writing since he was a child. From an early age he was exposed to older, original horror movies. The great ones that have made a mark in history. He also tackled reading the likes of Stephen King, Clive Barker, Ray Bradbury, Kurt Vonnegut, Dean Koontz, Charles Dickens, Harper Lee, H.G. Wells, W. W. Jacobs, etc. Thus, he decided to engage himself and write horror and dark fantasy, scaring readers such as his parents, his friends, a handful of neighbors, and even leaving a few school teachers scratching their heads wondering if the boy should be committed or not with his gruesome tales of terror. Short story ideas continued to visit. A book idea or two sometimes stopped by for a sit. In 2007 he decided to take a more professional approach with his work. Hence, as a member of the Horror Writers Association, already having five books published by small presses with more in the works, nearly twenty-five short stories published, adding to the few anthologies and collaborations with other authors, Brick Marlin trudges onward, hoping to achieve more creations, living in the minds of his characters making decisions such as whether to turn the knob and enter through the Red Door, or perhaps try and take a chance at the Blue Door, the one that is already ajar, a bony finger beckoning the next visitor.

James William Peercy spent his early years in California, (fifteen minutes from Disneyland!). As to the effect of this experience, we can only guess, but imagination makes the top of the list. His later years in Texas, he holds a BA in Computer Science with a minor in Math. Although analytical, the creative side has to find a way out. To ease the pain, he designs websites, programs code, and writes. If you like the book, drop him a line. If you don't like the book, drop him a line anyway. He will appreciate the feedback. As in the words of J.R.R. Tolkien, 'May the hair on your toes never fall out!'

11113280R00107

Made in the USA
San Bernardino, CA
07 May 2014